~THE~ MYSTERY
OF PHEASANT COTTAGE

PATRICIA ST JOHN

10 Publishing
a division of 10 ofthose.com

Copyright © 1977 by Patricia St John

This edition first published in Great Britain in 2018

The right of Patricia St John to be identified as the Author of this Work has been asserted by her in accordance with the Copyright, Designs and Patents Act 1988.

British Library Cataloguing in Publication Data
A record for this book is available from the British Library

ISBN: 978-1-785062-90-2

Cover design by Luther Spicer Internal design and layout by Author & Publisher Services

Printed in the UK

10Publishing, a division of 10ofthose.com
Unit C, Tomlinson Road, Leyland, PR25 2DY, England

Email: info@10ofthose.com
Website: www.10ofthose.com

1

Looking back now, I often wonder why I did not ask questions sooner, for I was aware of some mystery surrounding my life from a very early age.

I think this awareness arose from the fact that, although no one had ever told me so, I knew quite well that I had not always lived at Pheasant Cottage on the borders of the Eastwood Estate. Far, far back there had been somewhere else, where skies were bluer, and a very tall man had carried me in his arms. I remembered perfectly well that he had once gone down on all fours and let me ride on his back. As I grew older I used to wonder if he could have been my father but, strangely, I never asked.

I can remember too the first time I really began to wonder. It was eleven o'clock on a May morning. I was at infant school, sitting with my friends under the apple tree in the playground. We were drinking mugs of milk. A warm breeze was blowing, tossing the pink blossom petals on to our hair, and beyond the asphalt stretched the lawn starred with daisies. Everything was perfect until Harvey Chatterley-Foulkes, the bank manager's son, suddenly fixed his goggle eyes on me from over the rim of his mug and said loudly,

"Lucy, why do you live with your granny? Why don't you have a mummy and daddy?"

I looked round hopefully for Teacher, because I knew she would help me. But Teacher had gone to look for Jeremy who liked to hide behind the roller towel in the cloakroom and eat lollipops, and we were all alone. All the other children were looking at me now, and I had to think of an answer quickly. I stared defiantly at Harvey

3

and thought he looked like a fat frog, but not nearly so interesting.

"Because I don't," I replied. "Wipe your mouth, Harvey. You've got a milk moustache." This was what Granny said to me nearly every day, and so saying it usually made me feel confident and grown up. But Harvey took no notice.

"But why not?" he insisted. "I mean, where are they? Everyone has mummies and daddies. I mean, someone must have borned you!"

There was silence. If I said, "I don't know," they would all laugh at me and I should cry. Every eye was turned on me. Already I could feel the tears welling up.

"Perhaps they're dead," said Mary Blossom cheerfully.

"Or p'raps they ran away and left you," breathed Janie who read quite grown up storybooks.

"Or p'raps they're divorthed," broke in Bobby, who apparently knew all about it.

I looked round desperately and breathed a great sigh of relief, for Teacher was coming across the playground leading Jeremy, sticky and abashed. Everyone's attention was diverted, and I sidled up to her, slipped my hand into hers and felt safe. But Harvey was still determined to get to the bottom of my private affairs.

"Teacher," he squeaked excitedly, "*why* does Lucy live with her granny? I mean, why hasn't she got a daddy or…?"

Teacher's clear voice cut across his question.

"If I had a granny like Mrs Ferguson I shouldn't care if I had parents or not. She's as good as a father and mother rolled into one. You're a lucky girl, Lucy. My granny died when I was a baby… Wipe your mouth, Harvey, you've got a milk moustache. And now, everybody listen… as it's the first of May…"

She paused dramatically, apparently enjoying the little shiver of happy expectancy. My parentless state was completely forgotten. What wonderful event was about to take place, because it was the first of May?

"Because it's the first of May," repeated Teacher, "instead of going back to the classroom for arithmetic, we'll all go for a nature walk up to the spinney on the hill, and pick kingcups. They are right out."

There was a shout of joy. Sixteen 5- to 7-year-olds skipped, ran or danced towards the meadow. Teacher strode behind because she knew she would easily catch them up on the hill. I trotted quietly beside her, still holding tightly to her hand and feeling rather shaken. I knew now that the question had been there for a long time, buried deep and never asked. Now, all of a sudden, everyone had asked it, and there was no answer.

"I'll ask Granny today," I said to myself, and then forgot all about it in the delight of the outing. Teacher was in front now because the hill was steep for small legs. She looked like the Pied Piper with all her class puffing and hurrying behind her, while she called back exciting instructions.

"See how many different kinds of wild flowers you can find… I said different kinds, Sally, not all dandelions. Look very quietly in the hedges. You might see a nest… Harvey, stop chattering! We want to listen to the birds, and you are frightening them all away. Now, stand still, everybody… you too Betsy, stop jumping up and down! Now very quiet… Can anyone hear that thrush singing?" Then we plunged into the oak wood, and I was the first to spy a gleam of gold in the shadows and to cry out that I'd seen kingcups.

Everyone broke into a charge through the undergrowth but Teacher shooed us all back onto the path, because last year Timothy Williams had lost a shoe in the swamp and his mother had made such a fuss. But there were plenty of flowers to be reached from the path and presently we turned home with muddy feet and pollen-powdered noses. Teacher's shoes were the muddiest of all, from running up and down on the edge of the marsh in her efforts to stop us falling in to it.

Parents were waiting, and one by one the children dispersed, clasping their golden bunches. But I lived a good way out, and had my dinner at school. It was four o'clock before Teacher put me on the school bus. As we waited, she picked some blossom petals out of my hair and tied back my curls from my face. Then she suddenly stooped down and kissed me, and I wondered why, for she had never done such a thing before. Perhaps it was something to do with the question. Perhaps she was sorry for me.

Granny was standing at the bus stop with Shadow, our big, black Labrador, straining at his lead, and barking for joy because he knew I was coming. We usually chased each other madly home, with Granny, staid and upright, walking behind. But Shadow must have been disappointed that afternoon because I did not feel like playing. I walked quietly beside Granny, hugging my kingcups. And then, suddenly, I asked my question.

"Granny, why do I live with you and Grandpa? Didn't I ever have a mummy and daddy?"

It seemed very quiet after I'd spoken. I could hear a bee buzzing in the lilac and a blackbird whistling. At last Granny answered.

"Your mother was our dear daughter Alice, Lucy. She died when you were a tiny baby. There was no one else to look after you, so Grandpa and I took you as our own little girl."

"But didn't I have a daddy?" I persisted. "And why didn't he look after me? Is he dead too?"

There was a long silence while I waited confidently for the answer, because I knew that Granny was very strict about speaking the truth.

"He went right away," said Granny slowly, "and we never saw him again. He was not a good man, Lucy, and he could not have looked after you. You belong to us now, and always will, just as though you were our own little girl. Look, there's Grandpa! He's seen us."

We had reached our garden, and by the way she changed the subject and pressed her lips together, I knew that I was not expected to ask any more questions ever again. I did not mind. Beyond the beds of massed wallflowers and forget-me-nots, the front door of our cottage stood open and a delicious smell of baking came from the kitchen. Grandpa waved from his potato patch, his rosy face beaming a welcome. Above the chimney pots towered the feathery beech trees on the border of the Eastwood Estate. And I knew that beneath them lay cool, shadowed pools of bluebells, foamed with cow parsley. Home was a perfect place. What did I want with a father? Let alone a bad one!

Yet somehow that old far-away memory puzzled me, and the puzzle grew with the years. For if that tall man had been my father, then he could not have been wholly bad, or he would not have held me in his arms, nor would he have gone down on all-fours and let me ride on his back. But it was a riddle without an answer, and for five whole years I never mentioned it again to anyone.

2

Those five years passed swiftly. Anyone else might have called them quite uneventful, but to me they seemed packed with excitement. I moved up into primary school, got into the under-11s netball team, and came top of the class in English every term. I discovered the beauty of poetry and began to scribble stories in exercise books. Grandpa had bronchitis and went to hospital, I had measles, and the cat had kittens several times. I became a Brownie, and then a Guide, and when I was 11 years old, I went to camp.

But all these interesting, and mostly pleasant, events had nothing to do with my own real, secret life. For to me, the passing of time was not marked by terms and holidays, but by the appearance of the first primrose on the stream bank, or the sheathed bud of the first wild daffodil piercing the crumbling oak leaves. Summer was the song of the first cuckoo and the unfolding of the wild roses. Autumn was the blazing colours of the leaves, and the smell of bonfires. Winter was my own, solitary footprints over the white wastes of the Beacon. This was my real life, and so important to me that I had never much minded being an only child, or not doing the things that the other children did.

Sometimes, when the girls at school laughed at me because I'd never seen the sea, I would grow restless and wonder whether I would ever travel, or move beyond the familiar circle of school and home and church on Sundays. I did not see how I could, because my grandparents were growing older every year. Grandpa, who had been head gardener at the castle on the Estate for 30 years, only had a small pension. They were perfectly content to remain in their cottage and, apart from occasional visits to relatives in Birmingham, they had no wish to take holidays. They could not, in any case, because of the poultry. And, except when my friends made fun of me, I was content, too; content to play in the woods and climb the hills, to read and to scribble stories. These stories were always about children who went on long journeys, and travelled in ships and planes to all the golden countries I learned about in my geography book. I had my own duties in the cottage and garden too, and the days never seemed long enough.

Sometimes Mary Blossom, my best friend, came to spend the day and I would take her on to the Estate. But Mary was a stout, practical child who preferred to arrive somewhere than just to wander. Her often-repeated question, "Where are we going, Lucy?" annoyed me, as my unvarying reply no doubt annoyed her: "We're not going anywhere. We're just walking!" And after a time we would turn back, and skip or play games in the garden. I loved Mary dearly, but she belonged to my school world, and my woods bored her.

But from all the happy memories, one event stands out, clear and unforgettable: the Whitsun Guide Camp in the Cotswolds when I was 11. When Granny told Captain that I could go, provided I did not leave my vest off, or bathe in a river with a current, I was so excited that I hardly slept for two nights. And when we actually set off in the bus with our rucksacks and bedding, I could barely speak. I sat squeezing my clasped hands between my knees, bottling up my joy, because living with elderly people had made me rather a quiet child. But gradually, as we travelled through leafy lanes, sun-drenched landscapes and villages where the houses were built of brown stone and thatch, I relaxed. We sang, we chattered, we giggled, and we ate sandwiches and drank lemonade out of bottles. Then we were there, high on a hill at the margin of a great beech wood, overlooking the Gloucester plain, and Captain and Lieutenant were showing us where to put up our tents, and how to light a fire.

That holiday came up to my highest expectations in every way. I shared a tent with Mary. Every waking hour was thrilling, from the moment we crawled out into the sweet-smelling morning to the moment we snuggled into our sleeping bags in the dark, clutching each other in mock terror when the owls hooted in the woods behind us. But I remember most vividly the early morning when I woke before anyone else and, slipping on my jumper and shoes, crept out into the waking world. The sun had not long risen; a cuckoo called from the beeches. Captain was wandering about in a dressing gown and saw me.

"Lucy," she said, "would you like to dress and take a message to the farm for me? Straight through the wood and climb over the stile and cross the hayfield. You'll find them milking the cows. Tell them to save us 15 fresh eggs and we'll fetch them later."

I was slipping on my dress when Mary's tousled head appeared out of her sleeping bag. She blinked at me.

"Where are you going?" she yawned. "Shall I come too?"

"No, no," I replied hurriedly, "I shan't be long. I've got to go to the farm with a message. I've got to go now, at once. You can come and meet me if you like." I shot outside for this was my special expedition and I had to go alone. The sun had reached the level of the beech boughs and was flooding the aisles of the wood with radiance so bright that I could see nothing beyond. I seemed to be running into a clearing of light. Then the wood ended and I climbed over the stile and saw the hayfield, a tangled mass of flowers: moon daisies, campions, sorrel and buttercups, all dew-bedecked and sparkling.

I went crazy! I flung my shoes backwards over the stile and leaped and danced barefoot along the path, the flowers tickling my legs. I laughed, and clapped my hands, carried away with the joy of being alive on such a morning, loving the feel of the cold grass between my toes. Then, having delivered my message, I turned back and walked more slowly to prolong this beautiful, lonely hour. But it was not to be. Mary was trotting towards me, and by the look on her round face, I knew she had a secret to tell me.

"Lucy," she began mysteriously, "do you know what?"

"What?".

"Well, I came to meet you through the wood, and Captain and Lieutenant were standing by the stile."

"So what?"

"Well, they *saw* you!"

"I don't care."

"Yes, but Lucy, they talked about you. I heard them. They didn't see me, cos I waited behind a tree. I *heard* them, Lucy."

I was silent, my curiosity thoroughly aroused, but I wasn't going to show it.

"Lucy, shall I tell you what they said about you?"

"What, then?"

"Captain said," and here Mary's voice changed to a high ladylike drawl. "'Fancy good little Lucy going all wild like that! There's more in that child than meets the eye.' And Lieutenant said, 'Oh, Lucy's got plenty in her.

Her teacher says her essays are brilliant. She needs to get away from those grandparents of hers occasionally, and start living.' That's what they said, Lucy. There was more but I can't remember it all. And anyhow, they turned round and saw me."

"How silly!" I replied, rather crossly. "I live just as much as they do." But somehow the sparkle had gone out of the day, and all that morning while we breakfasted, and tidied, and bathed in the river, I puzzled over their remarks. What was wrong with being good? And what was wrong with my grandparents? And what had I been doing all these 11 years except living? I supposed that they said it because I hadn't done all the things the others had done, and because I'd never been to the sea. But after all, they knew nothing about my real life, and they'd never even set foot in the Eastwood Estate. I felt rather cross and superior all day, and they must have wondered what was the matter with me, until the delight of cooking sausages on the campfire drove the whole thing out of my mind.

But it had stirred up all the old questions. I was different.

That night I lay awake for a long time, with Mary snoring beside me, and listened to the owls and the rustle of the beech leaves. I tried to remember the face of the tall man who had gone down on all fours. But it was no good. It had gone for ever.

3

Whitsun camp was over but time sped on so fast that I seldom looked backwards or forward, but just enjoyed each new day. Once again summer blazed into autumn and this year I moved up into secondary school.

Once again the snow fell and blanketed the hills. Again I collected fir cones, and roasted chestnuts, and made secret Christmas presents. Again I heard the bleat of the first lamb at twilight, and smelt the warm south wind stirring the buds, and knew that spring was on the way.

And then it was the last day of the Easter term and the world was a great, singing chorus of green, and gold and blossom. Proper lessons were over and everyone was fidgety and longing for the holidays. Miss Bird, our English teacher, was reading us a poem, but the window was wide open. We could hear the ringdoves cooing, and the sheep calling their lambs. Miss Bird was getting little attention.

Miss Bird closed the book, stepped to the chalkboard and wrote "SUMMER HOLIDAY" in large letters. There was a slight stir of interest. A few heads were lifted.

I thought Miss Bird looked like summer itself, standing there in her yellow pullover in a pool of sunshine. "You will be planning your summer holidays soon," she announced, "so this is a competition for you to try this holiday, and next term there will be a prize for the best entry. You can write a story, or tell about what you did last year, or what you plan to do this year. Anything you like, but try to get the feeling of summer into it."

She looked round at our blank faces. "The feeling of summer seems to be rather a sleepy one," she said with a smile. "Let's collect some ideas and write them on the board. Mary, when I say, 'summer holiday', what do you think of?"

Mary jerked to attention. "Er…" she began, "Er… hot… and… ice creams…"

"Yes, all right. Somebody else? Jennifer?"

"Bathing… the beach… donkeys…"

"Punch and Judy show… bingo…"

"Tennis."

"Camping in our caravan."

"Riding my pony…"

Miss Bird was writing rapidly. She turned and faced the thoroughly awakened class.

"Yes, that's right, but what about the places you go to? Anna, where did you go for your last summer holiday?"

"We toured Scotland in our car."

"And what was Scotland like in the summer?"

"Oh, mountains and lakes, and it rained and the car broke down. We saw some castles, and battlefields and things. We watched for the Loch Ness Monster all one day, but no luck!"

Miss Bird gave a small sigh and looked at me.

"Lucy?" she asked.

Somebody gave a little titter, and Mary Blossom sprang to my rescue. "Lucy never goes away," she explained. "Her grandparents can't take holidays because—"

"That will do, Mary," interrupted Miss Bird. "Summer is here at home too, not just in the holiday places. Besides Lucy *did* go on holiday. She went to the Whitsun camp. Can you tell us about summer in the Cotswolds, Lucy?"

I closed my lips tightly and scowled at my teacher. Why should she ask me? She knew I never went anywhere. Then I glanced at her face and realised she was not making fun of me at all. She really wanted my help. She and I felt the same about summer, and she was appealing to me. I stared out of the window and tried to remember. Summer in the Cotswolds!

"The smell of honeysuckle and new-mown hay," I began slowly, "and that sort of shiny light coming through the beech leaves at sunset so all the leaves looked separate… seeing stars through a hole in the canvas… and the dew on the flowers in the early morning all sparkly… and bathing in the river… kingfishers came out of a hole in the bank and we swung on the willow branches…" Memories were flooding up, and I could have gone on for ever. Then I suddenly noticed the astonished faces of the other girls gaping at me, and I blushed and stopped short. Miss Bird had her back to us, and I had never seen her write so fast before. The silence was broken by the bell and a joyful clatter of chairs. It was time for break.

"You really did save the situation," said Mary admiringly. "I just couldn't think of anything but ice creams. I can't think how you manage to be so poetical, Lucy! I should think you'd get the prize easily."

I doubted it, for how could my Cotswold experiences compare with touring Scotland in a car, or even going to the sea? I felt restless as I wandered home from the bus stop that afternoon. I had recently been studying a poem called "The Forsaken Merman", all about the sea. I wished I could see the sea!

Now the salt tides shoreward flow,
Now the wild, white horses play,
Champ and chafe and toss in the spray…*

---

* Written by Matthew Arnold 1822-1888

What did they look like, I wondered, and where did they come from, those great tides? I felt a strange stirring at the heart of me, a reaching out for change. I opened the gate and walked up the garden path, so absorbed in my thoughts that I failed to call out my usual greeting. I stepped quietly into the passage. I was about to enter the doorway of the room where my grandparents were sitting with their backs to me, and I could not help hearing what they said. And having heard, my heart seemed to miss a beat, and I stood as though turned to stone.

"But Elsie," said my grandfather gently, "she will have to know soon. She is 12 years old, and after all, he is her father."

"But not yet, not yet," cried my grandmother. "There are still almost two years to go. Anything may happen in two years."

I stepped back very softly and crept out through the front door. They must not know that I had heard. I wanted to run away and hide in the wood, and think and think. But Shadow spied me from the kitchen, and came charging to meet me, slobbering on my feet, wagging his tail and jumping up to kiss me. There was nothing for it but to step back inside, just in time to see Granny fold a letter and slip it into the top drawer of her bureau. But they greeted me as usual and I helped to get tea, and we sat down to my favourite meal of ham salad with potatoes. The sun streamed in at the west window through a lattice of larch boughs, and made patterns on the wall. It should have been a happy, chatty tea as we caught up on the news of the day, but somehow we were all strangely silent. It seemed as though some shadow had come between us and I was almost glad when the meal was over.

"Any homework tonight?" asked Granny.

"No," I answered. "Tomorrow's the last day of term – and only a half day, Granny – so we don't do proper lessons. Can I go out for a bit when we've washed up?"

She looked at me with a strangely tender expression. "Grandpa and I will see to the washing up tonight, love," she answered. "You run along now, with Shadow. It's a beautiful evening. Come back before sunset."

Grandpa walked to the gate with me and asked where I was going, but I just pointed vaguely up the hill. I wanted to get away by myself, and I sped up the steep slope to the left of the house and flung myself into an old grassy trench where the Ancient Britons were meant to have made a last stand against the Romans. Shadow came and rested his nose against my arm. Within reach of my hand, small bracken fronds were unfolding like babies' fingers. In front of me, over the rim of the trench, lay the great plain, bathed in the last light. Every road was lit up by the sunset and seemed to run purposefully to the horizon. Every river was a shining ribbon. It looked like a bright clear map, and I suddenly realised what a vast place the world was. So many roads leading away from the safe shelter of my little home – such far, far distances!

What was I to do? If I asked, they would probably not tell me. Anyhow, they didn't want me to ask. But I had to know, because he was my father, and I was his daughter, Lucy. Besides, I was 12, old enough to be trusted. Even Grandpa recognised that, but Granny always had the last word, so that didn't help. Then as I lay there, chewing a bracken shoot and watching the sun sink towards the far Welsh mountains, an idea came to me. I was a bit shocked at myself, to be honest. I had never deceived my grandparents before, and that's what I intended to do tonight.

I would stay awake until my grandparents were asleep, and then I would creep down, find the letter in the drawer, and read it. I would see the address, and find out where my father was, and what it was all about. Of course, I knew perfectly well what Granny thought about people who eavesdropped, and looked at letters that didn't belong to them. But I decided it just couldn't be helped.

"After all," I argued with myself, "this letter does belong to me, really, because it's my father." Then I realised that the sun was sinking below the rim of the world and I jumped up, and raced down across the slippery grass, scattering the sheep in all directions. Grandpa was at the gate, peering short-sightedly down the road.

Evenings at the cottage were cosy times. We sat around the fire in winter, but on warm spring evenings we sat by the open window. I knitted or stuck in my stamps, while Granny read aloud, mostly from the shabby old books she had loved as a child: *Jackanapes, The Secret Garden, Heidi* and *John Halifax Gentleman*. At this time, we were halfway through *David Copperfield*, and Dora and Steerforth and the Pegotty family had become part of my life. I could hardly wait from evening to evening to hear the next instalment.

But tonight I did not want to sit quietly with my grandparents in the soft circle of light, as though there was nothing the matter. I felt outside the circle, a deceiver, and the loneliness of it was almost more than I could bear. To their great surprise and disappointment, I pretended to be sleepy and crept miserably up to my bedroom.

4

How was I going to keep awake? This was my big problem. If I could have stayed dressed it would have been easier. But I had to get into bed, because Granny always came to say goodnight to me, and to make sure that I'd folded my clothes properly and said my prayers. I always said my prayers, either "Our Father in heaven" or the old baby one Granny had taught me when I was 4: "Jesus, tender Shepherd hear me". They took about twenty seconds each. The saying of them had become such a habit that they meant nothing to me at all.

But tonight, as I ducked down on my knees, something seemed wrong. For the first time, I really thought about what I was saying. Could I say "Forgive us for doing wrong" when I was just about to do wrong by sneaking a look at Granny's letter? I switched over to "Jesus, tender Shepherd" but it was no better.

Let my sins be all forgiven,
Bless the friends I love so well.

I gave it up, and jumped into bed, and a moment later Granny appeared. But she did not glance at my folded clothes or mention my prayers. She put her hand on my forehead and asked if I felt all right.

"Yes, thank you," I answered.

"Are you sure, Lucy?" She lingered, as though loath to leave me. "Have you a headache? How about a drink of hot chocolate?"

This was supposed to be a big treat, but my stomach seemed tied in knots, so I just smiled, shook my head and closed my eyes. She went away slowly and I knew she was watching me from the door. But at last I heard her footsteps going downstairs, and then I sat up and looked round.

Perhaps an exciting adventure story would help keep me awake. I dared not switch on the light but I had a torch and, by its light, I tiptoed to my bookcase. I turned the pages of one book after another, but nothing seemed exciting except the letter in the bureau. All adventure seemed tame compared with the adventure of creeping downstairs and solving the mystery of my own life. I sat down by the open window and leaned my arms on the sill. The scent of growing things rose like incense in the warm dark – spring shoots growing upright, closed to darkness and open to light – and my heart ached. A screen of larch trees sheltered us from the windy hills. The night seemed to throw a mantle round our safe little home and Granny, Grandpa and me, so secure, so happy... till now. Why did this mysterious shadow have to come between us and spoil everything? I nearly decided to forget about that letter, to cuddle down and go to sleep... but no! I *must* find out, and this was probably my last chance. I leaned against the wall and dozed for a little, and then I woke with a start, for my grandparents were coming upstairs.

I had a funny feeling that Granny would come in and check on me. I dived into bed and, as I had expected, she came in and stood over me, with a torch in her hand.

"She's gone off all right," I heard her whisper, "but mark my words, Herbert, there's something the matter with the child."

I could hear Grandpa's distressed murmur, and the click of their door shutting. Another eternity, when I staggered up and down in my room, swaying with sleep, and then the line of light under their door disappeared. In another ten minutes or so I listened at the keyhole. I could hear Granny's steady snoring and knew that my time had come.

I tiptoed downstairs, and boldly switched on the light in the living room. I was shivering with guilty excitement as I pulled open the drawer. The letter I wanted was not lying on the top. Granny must have hidden it, and I had no idea what it looked like, so I thumbed through the pile, glancing at the addresses. They were mostly bills or letters from Granny's sister in Birmingham, or Grandpa's nephew in Stockton-on-Tees. There was nothing mysterious until I had nearly reached the bottom of the bundle. And then I saw an unusual sort of letter with the address printed at the top: "His Majesty's Prison, Greening."

I stood frozen, rooted to the spot, staring at the address. Only after a long time did my eyes move down to the actual letter and I saw who it was from – John Martin.

"Dear Mr and Mrs Ferguson," it began. "As the time of my imprisonment will soon be drawing to a close, I am writing to you on the subject of the guardianship of my daughter, Lucy. I am very grateful…"

I was so absorbed by what I was reading that I had ceased to notice anything, even the footsteps on the stairs and the opening of the door. It was only when he was right in front of me that I became aware of Grandpa, and realised that I was caught in the act. I thrust the letter behind my back and burst into frightened, defiant tears.

"Lucy, Lucy, my dear child, whatever is the matter?" whispered Grandpa, shutting the door very cautiously, as though we were hatching a plot together. I gulped and looked at him pleadingly. I suddenly realised that there was nothing to be afraid of. This was no policeman catching a criminal red-handed, but a distressed little old man in a very shabby dressing gown, who couldn't even see what I was doing because he'd left his spectacles upstairs. He peered at me short-sightedly.

"You're shivering, child," he said. "I'm going up to your room to get a blanket. Put on the kettle, my dear, and let's have a cup of tea."

A cup of tea was Grandpa's cure for all ills. He came tiptoeing down in a few moments and wrapped me up warmly. I stopped shivering and hiccuping, and relaxed. I could see that he was very anxious not to wake Granny, and not until we were both sipping steaming cups of tea did he remember to ask me what I was doing.

He had not noticed the letter at all. He had merely seen the light shining from the window and crept downstairs to turn it out. But my secret was too heavy and shocking to carry alone any longer. I needed Grandpa's help, and I leaned against him and told him all about it.

"You see, Grandpa, I know it's wrong to read other people's letters, but I *had* to know. He's my father, and I'd always wondered, only Granny would never tell me."

"No, it wasn't right," said Grandpa. "And I'm glad I came. Maybe we should have told you sooner, or maybe you should have asked us again instead of trying to find out alone. But in any case, it's high time you knew, although there is nothing to be afraid of. There is still quite a long time to go, if he does the whole sentence. By that time you'll be nearly 14, and you'll be allowed to choose for yourself. I don't reckon any court of law would force you to go with your father against your will. We can't stop him seeing you, but he can visit you here."

"But does he want me?" I asked. "I only saw the beginning of the letter and his name."

"Well now, yes, he seems to want you," replied Grandpa, gently taking the letter out of my hand. "But we've consulted lawyers, Lucy, and he couldn't take you from here… unless you wanted to go, which, of course, you wouldn't. He wouldn't be anything of a guardian for you. In fact, I'm afraid he's a very bad man."

"What did he do?" I asked. "Was I there?"

"Yes," said Grandpa, and he spoke very sadly. "It all happened after you were born and after our dear, dear Alice died. She met him at a friend's house, and he courted her. But your grandmother, she felt it wasn't right, and she wouldn't agree to their engagement. He was an unsettled kind of chap, so they just ran away and got married on their own. They went to Spain. He had a guest house there, I believe, and we never saw our daughter again. She died when you were born."

Grandpa's voice trailed off sorrowfully and he seemed to have forgotten about me. I gave his arm a small shake.

"I'm sorry, Grandpa," I whispered. "But what happened next? I mean, what happened to me?"

"We begged him to send you home to us, but he never so much as answered our letters. I believe he loved your mother very much and was heartbroken when she died. The second time we wrote, the letter was sent back to us. He had left that address and no one knew where he'd gone."

"But where was I, Grandpa? Did he take me with him?"

"Oh yes, but we don't know much about the next three years. I believe he drank a good deal, and got in with some drug business, helping to bring drugs up through Spain into France. Then he came back to England and the police were waiting for him. It was all in the papers. But to tell you the truth, Lucy, I didn't rightly understand it. It was about that time that he brought you to us."

"Oh! So he came here?"

"Oh yes. He arrived in a taxi, all unexpected like, with you in his arms, and asked us to look after you for a spell. I think he knew the police were on to him, but he didn't tell us so at the time. We had never seen you before, but there was no mistaking you. Such a funny little mite you were, and the image of your dear mother! The same thick, curly hair, the same grey eyes…"

"But my father, Grandpa! Did he love me?"

"Oh, yes. There was no doubt about that. You'd been well cared for too, and you talked a sort of mixture of English and Spanish. He said you'd had a Spanish nurse… he wouldn't stay, or tell us much. He just put you into Granny's arms. You clung to him and cried at first, but then you fell asleep. And when you woke up next morning you might have belonged to us all your life… you were just 3½."

"But tell me about my father, Grandpa. Didn't he ever come back?"

"No. A few days later it was all in the papers, and later he wrote telling us he'd got a ten-year sentence, and asking us to care for you. Your granny wasn't surprised. Said she'd known he was a bad lot from the beginning, and we must make sure you were never told. But when he comes out you'll have to know, Lucy, and maybe it's best you know now. But I sometimes wish that, for Alice's sake, we'd done things differently…"

"What was she like, Grandpa? My mother, I mean."

"She took after your granny, my dear. Your granny was the village schoolmistress when I married her, and there were many as said that she married beneath her. They were right, for I never had much book learning, but she seemed happy enough with me. We weren't too young and we only had but Alice, and she was so very much like your granny... Your granny always loved reading, but Alice, she had a passion for books and learning. She'd dance round the garden saying poetry to herself and be there under the rowan tree in summer, scribbling away. We managed to send her to college, too. She got a degree, but she couldn't stand to be long away from the cottage, and the hills. She was always coming back... until she met him... you're very like her Lucy, and we don't want..."

"Herbert, what in the name of heaven are you doing down there?" Granny suddenly called from the top of the stairs. We both jumped guiltily to our feet.

"I'm coming, Elsie," replied Grandpa, but I seized his arm.

"Are you going to tell her?" I faltered.

"Oh yes, of course," murmured Grandpa, hurrying to the door. I realised that he'd never had a secret from her in his life. I kept tight hold of his arm as we climbed the staircase.

"And *may* I ask what Lucy is doing?" Granny bristling with indignation, looked rather fierce and unfamiliar in her hair curlers. "Is there any reason...?"

"Yes, dear, there is... I'll tell you all about it... Lucy, go back to bed." And to my great astonishment, I saw Granny propelled speechless into the bedroom, and the door was slammed on me.

I climbed into bed, shivering, but it was a long, long time before I went to sleep. Wonder, shock, excitement, regret and a strange, cold fear of the future kept me awake. For one day this bad man was going to reappear and I was going to have to know what to do. I tossed and turned, till a cock crew far away and some sheep bleated up on the hill. A bird trilled the first few notes of the dawn chorus and, though the stars still blazed, another spring morning had begun. I was suddenly drowsy, and the confusion of my thoughts quietened. I just saw a man, heartbroken because his wife had died, kissing his baby daughter goodbye for ten years; sitting in a dark, lonely dungeon (for that was what the word "prison" made me think) and I'd never known. Perhaps I could have comforted him, even if he was such a bad man. I buried my face in my arms and wept. The next thing I knew, the sun was streaming into my bedroom, and Granny was standing by my bed with a cup of tea.

"Wake up, Lucy," she said. "I let you sleep on. But you'll have to hurry to catch the bus."

But I missed the bus and, as there was no afternoon school, my half day holiday became a whole day. As soon as we'd washed up the dinner things, Granny and I settled down in the garden. Then I heard exactly what Granny thought about children who sneaked downstairs at night to read other peoples' letters, and said they were sleepy when they were not. By the time she had finished we had rather lost sight of the main issue. I felt too crushed and ashamed of myself to ask any of the questions I wanted to ask.

"Sorry, Granny," I said, because that was what she expected me to say. And then I quite surprised myself by adding, "but I had to know sometime, didn't I, Granny? After all, he is my father, and I am 12 years old."

She stared at me, but the sharp answer I expected never came. "Lucy," she said and, to my amazement, her voice trembled, "I hope you will never have to have anything to do with him. No one could take you away from us now… not after all these years."

I stared back and saw that her eyes were full of fear – fear because she loved me, and because the shadow of losing me had hung over her, day and night, for about eight years. I flung my arms round her neck and hugged her. Then I ran off into the wood with Shadow at my heels.

It was quiet in the wood and now that the first shock of discovery was over, I wanted to think. Strange new thoughts were surging up inside me. I ran through the wood anemones and primroses to the edge of the trees where a sleepy stream ambled along, its golden water lingering round small rocks. All over the bank, wild daffodils pierced the dead oak leaves, and catkins pranced above me, scattering pollen on my hair. Here I sat, resting my chin on my knees, and realised I'd changed. Over the last 24 hours I'd begun to grow up in a hurry.

Granny was a very just woman. She always listened to what I had to say, and when she scolded me I usually knew in my heart that what she said was right. But today I was not so sure. I felt less ashamed of my "creeping and peeping", as she'd called it, than I had expected to, because it seemed to me that the letter hadn't really belonged to Granny at all. My father was mine, and the news belonged to me, and it was up to me alone to decide what I was going to do about it.

5

It was warm and peaceful where I sat; no sound but the gurgle of a brook in no hurry to move, and the muted excitement of nesting birds in the wood behind me. Then suddenly Shadow lifted his head and growled, and I turned to see a boy limping along the bank. He was a good-looking boy of about my own age, with thick brown hair, and green-hazel eyes set rather far apart in his heart-shaped face.

"Hi!" said the boy. "Have you got a handkerchief?"

I fished up the sleeve of my pullover and brought out a cotton hanky. He sat down beside me and held out his foot. It was badly cut and bleeding freely.

"Go down to the stream and hold it in cold water first," I said, remembering my Guides' first aid course. He obeyed, sitting on a stump and dangling his foot in the water. Then I tied it tightly with my handkerchief and we sat watching whether the blood would seep through or not. I had had little to do with boys since I left primary school, for I went to a girls' school. I was usually shy of them, but a boy in trouble was different.

"How did you do it?" I asked.

"I trod on some broken glass in the stream back there. I was paddling."

"But you're not supposed to be in the stream at all. This is a pheasant preserve and it's a private estate."

He smiled engagingly. "Then what are you doing here?" he asked.

"Oh, I belong here," I replied grandly. "My grandfather was head gardener at the castle for 30 years."

I added, "They always send him several brace of pheasant when they shoot."

"Really?" replied the boy. "But isn't it rather boring playing in this great place all alone? I mean, wouldn't it be more fun if there were someone else?"

I'd never really thought about it.

"Well, yes," I replied slowly, "I suppose it would. Do you often come here?"

"This is my first time. We've only just come to live here. I didn't come in through the gate. I came from the valley and I got under the barbed wire at the back. I belong to a natural history society at school and I'm doing a project on wildlife in this county. These woods are the best place to watch and I'm very careful about pheasants. I want to dam the stream lower down, to make a pool. Then more animals would come there to drink: specially early in the morning. Oh no! Look at my foot!"

The handkerchief was saturated with blood. Something had to be done at once.

"Where do you live?" I asked.

"Down in Eastbury. But I couldn't walk as far as that. I might bleed to death!"

"Well, come up to my house, and my granny will bandage it and phone for a taxi. We live by the main gate. It's only about ten minutes walk."

"Won't she mind? I'm a trespasser, remember."

"Oh no! She's not interested in pheasants. Grandpa is. But he's out in the garden, and he's so interested in his plants that he won't think to ask what you're doing. Come on!"

It took us nearly twenty minutes to reach the house, because the injured foot was very painful. Fortunately the boy had a knife, and we cut a stout thorn stick for him to lean on. He limped bravely along and as we walked, we talked, and I learned quite a lot about him.

His name was Donald, but he said I could call him Don, and he was 12 years old. His father had taken over the Royal Midland Hotel just before Christmas, and was making a success of it. He was obviously tremendously proud of his father. He hadn't any brothers and sisters, and went to boarding school, so he hadn't made many friends in the town yet. We had nearly reached home when he turned to me and said,

"And what about you? What were you doing all by yourself?"

"Oh, just thinking."

"Thinking? D'you often just sit and think? What do you think about?"

"Oh, nothing much. Here we are. This is our house."

"What a fantastic garden! D'you live with your grandparents?"

"Yes."

He stood for a moment, taking in the great drifts of daffodils in the grass, and the almond tree, heavy with blossom. I knew that he admired our cottage as much as I did. When he spoke again, it was almost wonderingly.

"Do you live here always? Where are your parents?"

"I haven't... well, I haven't really got any... my mother died... that's what I was thinking about. Look, there's Grandpa working on the rockery, and Granny bringing in the washing... Granny, I've brought someone. He's called Donald and he's hurt his foot."

Granny hurried across the lawn, brimming over with kindness and concern. In no time at all, Donald was sitting on a stool in the bathroom soaking his foot, and Granny was bustling round organising us all.

"I think that should be stitched," she said, surveying the ugly cut. "Can we phone your father, Donald, and can he fetch you? If so, Grandpa can go along to the phone box. Lucy, make a cup of tea, there's a good girl!"

"Oh yes, Dad's at home, and we've got a car," said Don, who had stopped bleeding. "I'll write down the number. Tell him where I am, by the big iron gates of the Estate. I'll be sitting on the garden wall waiting for him."

So Grandpa trotted off, and Granny bound up the cut, and I made tea in the sunny kitchen. Don soon hobbled downstairs, and drank a mug of tea. He also wolfed two pieces of Granny's chocolate sponge in a great hurry, because he didn't want to miss his father. Then we went out to wait on the wall in the early evening sunshine.

"Thanks a lot, Lucy," he said, "I really would have been in a mess without you and your gran. And they didn't say anything about the trespassing either."

"It isn't them," I replied. "It's the gamekeepers. They can be really nasty. But I was thinking… suppose you were with me…"

"If I said I was a friend of yours they'd let me come in, wouldn't they?" broke in Don eagerly. "I do want to dam that stream and make a big pool. How about helping me, Lucy, when my foot's better? Oh! Here's my dad!"

A car drew up sharply and the driver jumped out.

"What on earth happened, Don?" he began. "Can you walk? Where's the kind lady who rescued you?"

Granny came to the gate and said it was a pleasure, but the foot ought to be stitched. Don stood grinning from ear to ear, delighted with his adventure. Grandpa joined us with a bunch of daffodils and early narcissi, and we parted on the best of terms.

"Bye, Lucy," called Don, hobbling to the car, "I'll be seeing you!" And a few moments later they were off. I watched his waving hand until the car disappeared round the corner. Then I walked slowly back to the house. Granny stood in the doorway looking very pleased with herself.

"Lucy," she said, "I phoned your Guide Captain this afternoon. I thought you might like to get away for a little holiday over Easter. She says she can fit you into a Guide camp in Derbyshire for a week. Would you like that?"

I stared at her blankly. If she'd said this to me yesterday I should have gone crazy with excitement. But now… if I went away to camp I should never dam the stream or watch for squirrels in the early morning with Don. And if I wasn't there, he'd never be able to say he was my friend.

"I don't know, Granny," I answered slowly. "It's not as if they're girls from my school, is it? It was different, sharing a tent with Mary. I wouldn't know any of these girls, would I?"

"I guess you'd know them pretty well by the end of the week," retorted Granny, "but it's as you like. We don't want to get rid of you, do we, Grandpa? I just thought the holidays were kind of lonely for you here, but maybe you can ask your friends over."

"I'm not lonely, Granny," I answered quietly. "I'd rather stay for Easter. It's fun here at Easter, and I… well, I just don't want to go away."

So I stayed, and waited to see what would happen next. Four or five days later, Don reappeared on a bicycle with his foot well bandaged. I'd been to town with Granny on the bus, and we were all having tea when he turned up, so he came in and joined us. He got on very well with my grandparents. He had never had any, he explained, because his dad had been an orphan and his mother had come from South Africa, and he seemed to take it for granted that he could share mine. He ate a great deal, and then suggested we went to look at the stream.

It was the first of several happy mornings and evenings. They were the best time to watch wildlife, he said. Anyhow, he had a job, working for his dad during the day. He was saving up for a new bike. He was always anxious to get back by 9am, and seemed to think the hotel might collapse if he were late. But we dug out a pool big enough to wade in, from the stream bed, and dammed it. I would often hear his bicycle bell soon after sunrise. I would dress and creep down, explaining to a sorrowful Shadow that he could not come. Then we would run out into the light and blossom and birdsong and crouch in the bushes to watch birds, squirrels and rabbits. And once, on a never-to-be-forgotten early morning, when we were climbing a tree and not watching at all, we suddenly saw a vixen playing with her three roly-poly cubs. They tried to bite her tail but she cuffed them onto their backs, where they lay waving their little paws in the air and rolling over each other. At last they grew tired, and the mother lay on her side and let them suck. We sat motionless, watching from above, until the meal was over and the vixen trotted away through the daffodils, her babies trotting unsteadily behind her.

Our talk was seldom personal. He told me about birds and foxes and fossils and what his dad said and did, and I told him about 'The Forsaken Merman' and 'The Highwayman' and characters from books I'd read. It was halfway through the holidays before Don asked the question I dreaded, the question which always came up in the end and which I had never been able to answer. Now that I *could* answer, it was almost worse.

We were wandering home on a quiet, grey April evening, noticing things, as usual. I had stopped to look at the leaf fingers released from the horse chestnut buds, and Don was peering round through a pair of binoculars which his dad had given him for his birthday. I wished I had given him a birthday present, but I hadn't known about it.

"I can see that thrush right up close," he said. "I can almost count the speckles on her breast. Dad knew I wanted binoculars, and he bought me a really good pair." He turned to me. "Lucy, what happened to your dad? I know you said your mother died. Did he die too?"

Suddenly I realised that I no longer dreaded this question. I wanted to share my tangled thoughts with someone to whom I could speak quite freely without fear of hurting their feelings.

"Sit down on this log, Don," I said. "And I'll tell you all about it."

I told him everything, all about my past, and the letter, and creeping downstairs, all about Granny and Grandpa and their fears, all about the great big questions that kept me awake at night: "When he comes, what shall I do?"

"What would you do, Don, if your dad was a terrible man in prison, and yet he wanted you?" I asked finally.

And Don, tossing his thick brown hair back from his forehead, replied without hesitation, "I should find him somehow, somewhere, and I should say to him, 'I don't care what you've done, Dad. I'm still your boy!'"

6

We went home, and Don, after cadging a bun and a cup of tea off Granny, cycled away into the dusk as usual. But, once again, something had happened. Somehow, through that single sentence of Don's, I suddenly knew what to do. All my confused sense of right and wrong, my conflicting loyalties, seemed to have come to rest in that single sentence, as though it were a compass, pointing me home. Somehow I must find my father, or wait till he found me, and tell him that whatever he'd done, I was still his girl. For the first time, I felt I was starting out in the right direction instead of running round in circles. For the first time since I had read that letter, I fell asleep the moment my head touched the pillow.

Two days later it was Good Friday, and Granny, Grandpa and I went to the service in the little Norman priory that nestled against the fall of the hill, like an old grey rock washed by bright seas of daffodils. I quite liked going to church. I liked wearing my best clothes and singing hymns, and I loved the musty smell and the simple beauty of the arches and pillars. During the sermon I usually made up stories while Grandpa snoozed and Granny listened to the vicar. That day, though, it was a different sort of service. There was no sermon, just hymns and prayers, and I found myself listening, *really* listening. Then we sang a hymn I'd known since I was small, and I found myself thinking, *really* thinking, about the words: "He died that we might be forgiven, he died to make us good."*

* Cecil Frances Alexander 1818-95

If that was true, bad people could change and even prisoners could be forgiven. While I was still thinking about this, the service ended, and we streamed out of the cool, cave-like priory into the green and gold of the April morning. I wondered what it was like to come out of prison... to be forgiven... I walked home very quietly, still thinking hard.

That afternoon, I joined Grandpa who was thinning out seedlings, and weeded the bed beside him. I felt I needed to get every ounce of information that I could from him. And besides, I liked talking to Grandpa.

"Did my mother like gardening, Grandpa?" I began.

"Well now, I don't know that she did much. She loved wild, growing things, and wandering about, but she liked reading better than working in gardens. She was a great one for book learning, was Alice."

"And I'm really like her, Grandpa?"

He smiled very tenderly. "You might be her all over again, pretending to do a bit of weeding, and sitting back and talking instead. That was her way! It was, 'Dad this', and, 'Dad that'! I never got any work done when she was about."

"But aren't I like my father, Grandpa? Surely you can't be only like one parent?"

His smile faded. "I don't think you favour him at all, Lucy, and even if you did..." He paused, groping for words. "It's like this, or so it seems to me: if you cross a weak strain with a healthy strain, and then you take the seedlings and dung them, and water them, and shelter them and keep the slugs off 'em – well, they'll grow up healthy plants. The weak strain'll die out. We've tried to give you plenty of sunshine and shelter, Lucy..."

"And you've kept the slugs off me," I added with a giggle. "But Grandpa, don't bad people ever turn good? I mean, don't people ever change?"

Grandpa considered this for a long time.

"Well," he said at last, leaning on his spade, "even the Bible says something about not picking grapes or figs from thorn bushes… flowers is flowers and weeds is weeds, but people *can* change, by the grace of God. But prison's a poor soil, Lucy! They mostly come out worse than they went in! But there is the grace of God… you know what I mean by 'grace', Lucy? God's free favour… he can turn ugly things beautiful. But your granny knows more than I do. You'd best ask her about it."

He gave a deep sigh and stooped to his seedlings. I sighed too, and grubbed up a few more weeds, for Grandpa's answer had given me little hope or comfort. Then I glanced up, and noticed a heap of manure beside the tool shed, and gave a little cry of pleasure. Two white narcissi appeared to be springing out of it, although whether their bulbs were embedded in the dirt, or whether their spear-like sheaths had pierced it, I could not tell.

"Such beautiful flowers out of such dirty, smelly manure!" I said to myself. "It's like the grace of God. Ugly things *can* turn beautiful. I think bad people *can* become good."

I saw little of Don until after Easter, for he had been very busy helping his father, and the new bike was in view. He had earned quite a lot of money taking luggage up in the lift, working in the garden, cleaning the car, and running errands for Mr Smith.

"Who is Mr Smith?" I said idly. It was a warm, sleepy afternoon and we sat dangling our feet in the pool, eating our sandwiches and exchanging news. The daffodils were nearly over, but a faint impression of blue in the shadows heralded the arrival of the bluebells.

Mr Smith, explained Don, with his mouth full, was their one and only resident lodger. He'd taken an attic about ten days previously and was going to stay till the summer. He was a nice man who'd travelled in lots of countries – he'd been in an avalanche and seen a bullfight – but he wasn't very strong and he had a bad cough. Don liked talking to him, but wasn't allowed to disturb him much because he was always busy.

"What does he do?" I asked.

"He writes books," replied Don casually. "He's got a whole shelf of them, but he won't let me read them. He says…"

"Writes books!" I gasped. "Do you mean to say he writes real books – to be printed, and people read them?"

"Of course! What else would you do with books? Eat 'em?"

I gazed at him in wonder. He ran errands for a real live author, whose books were printed! I thought of the exercise books in my bedroom, filled with pages of happy scribble. But would I ever write anything that could be printed? And who would tell me how to set about it?

"I should like to meet Mr Smith," I said boldly.

"Actually," replied Don, "he'd like to meet you. I told him how you wrote stories and poems and things. He said he was interested in children who wrote things, and he'd like to see some of your pieces. Perhaps he'll come up to the woods with me one day when he's better, but I shan't be coming for a few days. Dad thinks there's some badgers in a little spinney off the Tewkesbury Road, and we're going to watch. They come out when it's getting dark."

"Wish I could see them," I said.

"OK," said Don good-naturedly, "but you can't come until I know they exist. If they are really there we'll try and fix something. Badgers are worth seeing."

He was as good as his word. He came peddling up the hill, very breathless and excited, about five days later, and burst into the kitchen where Granny and I were spending a peaceful afternoon baking.

"Please, Mrs Ferguson," he announced, "can Lucy come? Mum says she can have tea with us at home, and then she can come and see the badgers. We saw hundreds of them, Mrs Ferguson! Well I mean, we saw at least seven! It was pitch dark and we watched them dancing and boxing."

"May I ask how, in the pitch dark?" asked Granny dryly.

"Well, it got pitch dark as we watched," explained Don, "and it was pitch dark coming home in the car. When we first saw them it was sunset – the sky was all red, and we lay for ages waiting for them to come. You have to keep very, very still, Lucy. You mustn't move for about an hour."

"That must be quite a trial for you!" remarked Granny, observing Don, who was jumping around in excitement. "And who is going with you? Your father will take you, and bring Lucy back, will he?"

Don shook his head. "Dad's busy tonight," he explained. "He's got lots of guests. Mr Smith says he'll come with us. He's got a car, and he'll bring Lucy back by nine. OK, Mrs Ferguson? Oh, what fantastic cakes!"

"Sit down, Lucy and Don," smiled Granny, "and have some cake and lemonade. I want a word with Grandpa."

She was away some little time, and I discovered later that she had sent Grandpa hurrying off to the phone box to find out all about Mr Smith. As he seemed satisfactory in every respect she returned at last, and gave permission for me to go. I was wildly excited, already standing with one foot on the pedal of my bike, but whether at the prospect of seeing a badger, or of meeting a real live author, I was not quite sure.

Then we were off, speeding under the sweeping boughs of the larch trees, which leaned from high up the bank. I remember thinking there was no joy in the world like the joy of going downhill on a bicycle with the wind singing in my ears, and my hair blown backwards. At the bottom of the hill the meadows broadened out, and we skimmed into the town. We pushed our bikes across the cobbles of the old marketplace between the overhanging timbered houses. Don's hotel lay at the far end, and we went round the back to his parents' flat.

"Here's Lucy, Mum," said Don abruptly. He disappeared into the next room, leaving me smiling shyly at a stout, comfortable-looking woman, who greeted me with Don's engaging smile. She told me to sit down while she finished getting tea. We were having it early on account of the badgers, whose habits had to be timed very carefully. So I sat on the sofa while Don rushed round making preparations for the expedition. You'd have thought we were going to the North Pole from the fuss he made. And suddenly the door opened, and a voice said quietly,

"So you are Lucy, who writes poetry. Good evening, Lucy. I'm Mr Smith."

I leaped to my feet, and then tried hard not to show my disappointment. I had no clear idea of what I expected an author to look like, but certainly not like the man in the doorway. He was tall and thin with bowed shoulders, bald on the top of his head, and had a general look of weariness and ill-health. But I recovered myself quickly, for his face was very kind, and he looked at me with real interest. I smiled, and shook hands, and told him I was Lucy, and that I did write stories and poems and things but they weren't very good.

"They'll improve if you just keep writing," said Mr Smith. "You must bring them here one day, and let me see them. I believe it's teatime now; I'm invited too, as it's a sort of badger celebration party."

It really was a party with ham and salad, fruit and ice cream, and cake. Don's dad made all sorts of jokes and we laughed so much that it was nearing sunset when Mr Smith, Don and I finally set off. We were armed with a torch, binoculars, peppermints and a rug for Mr Smith, who was delicate. It was about a twenty minutes' drive through budding country lanes. But I hardly noticed where we were going because Mr Smith started talking to me about the books and poems I'd read, almost as though I were an equal. He knew all about *David Copperfield* and *The Wind in the Willows*, and 'The Forsaken Merman'. I found myself talking too, as I'd never talked to any other grown-up before. Then I remembered poor Don in the back. He was jigging up and down and dying to give us a lecture on badgers.

"They have their babies down in the setts about February," he began, when he could get a word in edgeways. "Here, this is where we stop, Mr Smith, up this little lane. You can leave the car in front of the farm. We have to go across that field and through that wood, and we'll have to hide in the nettle patch. The sett is just under those bushes. You'll need that rug, Mr Smith, because of your cough." He was hurrying across the field where the daisies were already closing their petals. The sky above the hawthorns was faint gold. As we approached the nettle patch he went down on all fours and motioned us to follow, and keep quiet.

I had a feeling that Mr Smith was not really used to creeping through brambles and nettles on all fours, but he did as he was told. We found ourselves in a rather uncomfortable little hollow, where we crouched and tried not to scratch our stings. It was rather cold and the dew was falling.

The brightness behind the trees faded, and the last lone thrush stopped singing. We lay so still that we could hear all sorts of unfamiliar little sounds: the flight of wings as a bird flew home, the thud of a rabbit's back legs in the field behind us. It was getting dark, and I suddenly felt glad of Mr Smith's presence in the ditch beside us. Don was leaning forward, breathless and absorbed.

And then it happened. A rustle in the dead leaves, a black nose with a gleaming white stripe... a large badger rose up in the dusk, sniffing the air. It lolloped a few paces, and another appeared. Then they turned face to face, and rose on their hind legs in a kind of grave twilight dance. Then came another and another. There was an old fat badger and two small, round, frolicsome badgers, tumbling clumsily about, scrambling up molehills, and rolling off again. We watched like statues; watched till the light had gone, and there was nothing more to be seen or heard, but ghostly shapes, and odd little coughs and snufflings, and the rustling of dead leaves.

Then Mr Smith sneezed. And in one second, we were alone with the chilly night, the damp ditch and the stinging nettles.

"I'm very sorry!" said Mr Smith.

"Don't worry!" said Don generously. "It was too dark to see them any more in any case. Wow! Weren't they fantastic, Mr Smith? Aren't you glad you came, Lucy? Bet you never saw anything as good as that before! Here, have a peppermint everybody, to warm you up! Don't step in that cowpat, Mr Smith. Race me to the gate, Lucy!"

He was in tremendous spirits, and chattered the whole way home. But I only half listened, because to me the evening had been an almost mystical experience. I knew that I should never forget it as long as I lived – that first thrusting of the striped snout, then another and another. We had reached my gate, and the moon was flooding the garden, making Grandpa's prize tulips look like pale lanterns.

"Goodnight, Lucy," said Mr Smith, "and tomorrow write about tonight. Write about the birds flying home, and the smell of the wet grass. Write what you felt when the first badger appeared… write about the moonlight on the tulips… write it all, and let me see it."

"All right," I said, jumping out of the car. "I'll try. Goodnight, and thank you very much!" And they left me standing by the gate, wondering how Mr Smith knew what I'd been thinking.

7

The days sped by, and the beginning of term put an end to Don's company. We said goodbye in the bluebell wood on a bright spring evening when the westering light, filtering through the young beeches, dappled the pools of blue. Don was perched on a fallen tree trunk, swinging his legs, when he made the disastrous suggestion.

We had been talking about my father again, for the situation had fired Don's imagination. He kept thinking what *he* would do if *his* dad were in prison.

"If I were you, Lucy," he remarked, "I'd run away and find him. Why don't you, Lucy? You know where the prison is. It's not very far. I think it's on the main line to London. You could probably get there and back in a day, and they couldn't stop you. All prisoners are allowed visitors. I asked my dad."

"I couldn't do that," I said rather crossly. "Granny would never let me. You know she wouldn't."

"You wouldn't tell her, silly," said Don. "You'd have to be going somewhere else, and then not go, and then go and see your father instead. You'd probably have to make up some sort of a story. But, after all, he's your father, isn't he? If it were mine, nothing would stop me!"

"But I never do go anywhere else," I objected, "and anyhow, I wouldn't have enough money, and it's wrong to tell lies, and how would I know the way?"

Don shrugged. "It could probably be worked out," he said. "Think about it, and I'll come and see you when I come home for the weekend, in three weeks' time. Bye, Lucy! Have a good term!" He gave me a warm, hopeful smile and darted off through the arches of the wood, leaving me trying to forget this most disturbing conversation. But the seed of an idea had been sown, and neither fear, reason, nor conscience could stop its growing.

At first it was easy to forget because going back to school was always exciting and eventful, and during the first week the result of the prize essay was announced at assembly. To my amazement, I, who had never been anywhere, had won the prize. I had to walk up and receive it, a book token. And, later on, Miss Bird read my essay aloud to the English class. I was thrilled, and so were my grandparents. I could hardly wait for Saturday to show Mr Smith.

I had started visiting Mr Smith at the weekend to show him anything I had written, and he, in his turn, gave me fresh books or poems to read. He often criticised and seldom praised, but this time he seemed pleased. He read my essay twice through, and smiled.

"That's the way, Lucy," he said. "You really experienced this, didn't you? What are you going to buy with your book token?"

"I don't know," I replied. "Granny said to ask you. Have you any ideas?"

"What about a good young people's anthology?" said Mr Smith, after thinking for a moment. "I should like to introduce you to some of the more modern poets. One of these days soon I shall be going into town to buy some books myself. Do you think your grandparents would let you come with me?"

"I'm sure they would," I said enthusiastically. "I'll ask them. Thank you very much, Mr Smith, I'd love to come."

But that seed of an idea was growing and beginning to fill my mind. In the daytime, I was absorbed with my lessons and interests. But the moment Granny had switched off the light and opened the window, my thoughts turned back to Don's suggestion. Some nights I lay awake till nearly midnight, tossing, turning and planning, for now something had happened that had brought the whole plan actually within the range of possibility.

There was going to be a Whitsun camp leaving early on Whit Saturday morning. We were going to Clee Hill in Shropshire, and we would pitch tents, go for a hike, sleep there, parade to church and come back on Sunday afternoon. The expedition wouldn't cost much but I wasn't sure I had enough money to pay for my train fare. I had very little pocket money, and my Post Office Savings book was locked away in Granny's cash box. Also, where could I stay the night? These two objections seemed impossible to overcome, so I gave a sigh of relief, and tried to forget about it once more. With a lightened heart I put down my name for Guide camp, and asked if I could share a tent with Mary Blossom again.

But after three weeks Don came home with easy solutions to all my insoluble problems. Money could be got somehow. He'd give me some himself, from his bicycle savings. In fact, he produced money from his pocket and handed it over with a flourish then and there. He said if I asked nicely he was sure Mr Smith would buy my book token. With my own money that ought to be enough, and the night was no problem either. He would be home for Whitsun. All I had to do was take the train to Eastbury, and go to the little spinney near the hotel and wait. He would come out every half hour and hoot like an owl so I'd know it was safe to come out. And he would put a blanket and pillow for me in the stable behind the house. No one ever went there in the evening, and there was plenty of straw for the horse. I could spend a delightful night there, with the horse, and wander about the hills the next day until it was time to go home. He would smuggle out some food for me, and all would be well.

He was swinging on the gate as he talked. The wind blew his thick hair back from his forehead. His eyes were alight with excitement. Nothing seemed impossible. And yet, I shivered with fright and misery! The spinney would be dark and lonely, and I'd never slept in the company of a horse before. Besides, what would I say when I got home, and my grandparents asked me if I'd enjoyed camp?

Even Don accepted that this last one was a real problem.

"I think, Lucy, you'll have to tell them," he said seriously. "After all, there's nothing all that bad in going to see your own dad, but it's better not to tell too many lies. If you told the truth *then*, the lies you'd told *before* wouldn't matter any more, would they? And in any case, that army person..."

"Captain," I corrected.

"That Captain person might meet your Gran and tell her you hadn't been to camp. Then you'd have had it, wouldn't you!"

"I *couldn't* tell them," I cried.

"Well," said Don patiently, "it's up to you, Lucy. I can't do any more for you. It won't be easy, it's true. But if it was my dad, I'd have a try!"

There was a fortnight to go, and the memory of it is rather confused. I only remember lying in bed and hearing the clock strike over and over again, waking heavy-eyed in the morning, and trying to eat when I had no appetite. Whitsun was creeping nearer and nearer, and I could not make up my mind.

I had the money, or would have when Granny gave me my fee for camp. Don had been most efficient in finding out when the train left and the price of a day return. On the Saturday before Whitsun, I took my book token to Mr Smith, and asked him to buy it, as he wanted some books himself. He had looked at me in astonishment, and I could see that he was disappointed.

"But why, Lucy?" he asked. "I thought you were going to buy that anthology. You shouldn't sell your prize."

"I know." I felt my cheeks grow crimson. "But you see, I need the money for something very badly. Please, Mr Smith, I really do!"

"Can't you tell me what for?"

I shook my head miserably.

"Do your grandparents know?"

"Not yet... I expect they will later."

"Is it for yourself, or for someone else?"

"For someone else."

"Is it for a present?"

"Sort of... not exactly."

"Lucy, couldn't you possibly tell me?"

"Not yet... I will later. I'll come and tell you on Whit Monday, Mr Smith, honest I will! And it's nothing really bad."

"Does Don know?"

"Yes, and he doesn't think it's bad either. He thinks it's something I ought to do."

"I see!" Mr Smith seemed to have quite a respect for Don's opinions. "Well Don seems a good lad, and I think you're a good girl too, so I'll trust you. And remember, on

Whit Monday you're going to tell me all about it. Here's your 7s 6d but I shall keep your book token here in my drawer. You mustn't sell that. It was given to you to buy books, not to sell."

Exhausted with relief, I leaned back in the armchair clutching the money in my pocket. Mr Smith began talking about Ancient Greece, and started to read me Tennyson's 'Oenone'. But about ten minutes later, he closed the book.

"You're not attending, Lucy," he said gently. "You're far away. I wonder what this big secret is!"

I couldn't concentrate at school either, and lost marks in all directions. Miss Bird, meeting Granny in town on Thursday, actually asked her if she thought I was quite well. They decided between them that I was worrying about my exams, that the Guide camp would probably do me good, and that I'd better have some vitamins.

But I knew that nothing could do me good, and time was running out fast. I came home from school on Friday evening to find all I needed for camp laid out neatly beside my little rucksack: clothes, bathing things, camp money and a big bag of sweets. The sweets I would give to my father, but what on earth was I to do with all the other things? I supposed I should have to carry them round on my back till I came home again. Things were getting worse and worse.

I lay awake for a long time, trying to decide what I should say on my return. I knew that Granny's pet hate in life was "a sly child". No full-grown fox could be slyer than I was being just then. Only one thought kept me from giving the whole project up. By the time I came home I should have seen my father, and beyond that fate would, no doubt, take over.

I slept fitfully, my sleep broken by strange dreams. I had reached the prison, and my father turned away from me… I was back, coming in at the gate, but my grandfather would not look up from his French beans. I awoke, drenched with perspiration. The birds were singing and the sun rising. No retreat now! The sooner I left the better.

Wearing my Guide uniform, with my rucksack on my back, I swallowed a hasty breakfast, and explained that I'd arranged to go to Mary Blossom's house early so that we could start together. Having started telling my miserable lies, I felt I wanted to be sick. For one safe moment I clung to Granny; her clothes smelt of lavender and mothballs, and the clasp of her arms was infinitely comforting. Then I remembered that I was a "sly child" and she might never feel quite the same about me again on my return… unless she need never know. I turned away and ran down the road without a backward look. My great adventure had begun.

Then I heard my name called urgently, and turned to see Grandpa, puffing terribly, trotting after me as fast as he could go. What could he want? I was shaking all over when he came up to me, but it was only to slip a coin into my hand, unseen by Granny who would have accused him of spoiling me. "For ice creams, Lucy," he panted, "or pop – or whatever you like. Have a good time, dearie."

It was the last straw. I snatched the money and turned away, the tears streaming down my face. But no retreat! There was just one more thing to be done, and then the big risks were behind me. I had written a note to Mary the night before, asking her to tell Captain that I was unexpectedly prevented from coming; I had to go somewhere else. It was a strange, vague little note, but by the time Captain received the message I should be far away.

I crept up to Mary's front door, slipped my note through the letter box, and darted back to the gate. But there was no escaping Mary. She saw me from the window and came bounding to the front door.

"Lucy, Lucy, wait for me," she yelled. "Why are you running on? We were going together!"

"I can't come" I shouted desperately. "I've got to go somewhere else. Read the note, and tell Captain."

"Can't come?" squealed Mary. "Why not, Lucy? You said you'd come! And if you're going somewhere else, why have you got your Guide uniform on? Lucy, Lucy... wait."

But I had no answer ready, and fled down the road, with Mary, too stout to follow at my speed, moaning at the gate. That's done it! I thought to myself. She'll tell Captain all about me, and they'll know there's something fishy. Perhaps she'll even get in touch with Granny.

But the bus was coming, and I jumped on and reached the station without any trouble. I went to the ticket office and asked for a day return to Greening, but having never done such a thing before, I could only speak in a whisper.

"Lost yer voice, luv?" said the man, leaning forward.

I repeated my request in a strange croak that seemed to belong to someone else.

"Over the bridge on number three," said the man. "Now don't lose your ticket and enjoy yer 'oliday!"

Down on the platform there was nearly forty minutes to wait. I ducked behind a large litter bin in case any of my teachers were going away for the weekend. But the coast seemed clear, and at last I actually found myself settled in a corner seat of a third class compartment with the train starting up. Then, for better or worse, we were off. I knew it took two and a half hours to get to Greening but, having no watch, I had no way of marking time. I amused or annoyed my fellow passengers by seizing my rucksack each time the train drew to a halt and asking, "Excuse me, but is this Greening?"

"Relax, ducks," said a kindly lady when this had happened four times. "I'll tell you in plenty of time to get off at Greening." And after that, I think I must have dropped off to sleep, because the next thing I knew she was shaking me gently, and we were drawing into what seemed to be an enormous station. She helped me on with the rucksack and opened the door for me. I stepped out and joined the crowd hurrying to the exit.

8

Only when I got outside the station and stood in the busy town street did I realise that I had no idea where to go. I dreaded asking anyone the way to the prison. They might guess my secret, or even think I'd done something wrong. This worried me so much that I wasted half an hour plucking up my courage until, in the end, I timidly asked a lady who had no idea where the prison was. Then I asked a boy, not much older than myself, who looked friendly. But he laughed, and asked me what I'd "been an' gone an' done", and how many years I'd got, and went off whistling.

It was well past one o'clock by now, and I was getting desperate. I was being jostled in the street, and yet I'd never before felt so completely alone. I looked round and saw an old lady selling flowers and, gathering up my courage, I crossed to her.

"Can you tell me the way to the prison?" I whispered shamefacedly.

"Prison, love?" she queried. "That's not far from here. Go up to the end of that street over there, and take the number 8 bus. It'll take you right close. Then ask again."

I ran all the way and jumped on a number 8 which was just passing. It was crowded and I had to wait for my ticket.

"Prison, dear?" said the conductor. "You're going the wrong way and this is a one-way street. You'll have to get off at the next stop, cut up Church Street and catch the number 8 going back. That goes right past the prison."

I could almost write a book about my misfortunes in Greening alone. I cut down Church Street instead of up it, and got lost for quite a time before I found the right bus stop… where I was told the number 8 had just gone. Standing in the road waiting, I realised I'd had no dinner and very little breakfast, and was desperately hungry. I trotted off to a shop and bought myself a bun, some chocolate and pop. But I took longer than I meant in choosing what I wanted, and when I got back I saw the next bus disappearing round the corner.

I knew by this time that I was unlikely to catch the train that Don had told me to catch, but this did not particularly worry me. For by the time I needed to decide anything, I should have seen my father. When the next bus rolled up I felt strengthened by the picnic and strangely at peace. Only a little longer, and I should hand over the responsibility of this wild expedition into my father's hands. He would tell me what to do.

"Prison up the top of the street next to the church," shouted the conductor, and I was glad to get off for I felt all eyes upon me. But as I hurried towards it, my heart was as light as air. I'd done it. I'd arrived! I thought of Don. "I don't care what you did, Dad," I whispered to myself. "I'm your girl, and I've come."

The entrance was quite obvious, an enormous door in a high stone wall and a smaller door with a grid set in it. The bell was out of reach – I was rather small for my age – so I knocked hard with my fists. No one answered at first, so I went on knocking, and my heart began to beat rather fast. Supposing visiting hours were over? I started kicking rather wildly and at last the grid above my head opened and a voice said, "Hello?"

"Hello," I answered, standing away from the door so as to be seen. "I've come to visit my father, Mr Martin. He's been here about eight years or so. I'm Lucy Martin, his daughter."

"Sorry," said a voice. "It's not visiting day today, and children aren't let in alone. Ask your mum to bring you next time."

I could hardly believe my ears! I simply stared as the grid closed, and then I panicked. I ran at the door, kicking, hammering with my fists and shouting at the top of my voice. "Don't go away! Please, please, don't go away. I haven't got a mother, and I've come alone... Oh, please let me in! He's my father!"

I didn't notice the passers-by forming into a little crowd to stare at me. But one lady who thought, no doubt, that my father had just been locked up, tried to persuade me to come away. I pushed her aside and continued my crazy assault and, in the end, she rang the bell above my head and the grid opened again.

"Can someone speak to this little girl?" said the lady. "She seems very much upset and quite alone."

I heard footsteps receding across the courtyard, and the lady put her arm round my shivering little figure, trying to quieten me. Then we heard the sound of footsteps approaching, a key turned in a lock, and the little door set in the big door opened. A large man in a navy blue uniform stood looking down at me. "Now, now!" he said. "What's all this fuss?"

"It's my father," I gulped. "He's here. I came all the way from Eastbury to see him and you won't let me in... and I don't know where to go now, and I think I've missed the last train home... and oh, please! I came all by myself... and I *must* see him. Please, please, please let me in!"

The warden looked down at me thoughtfully, and I'm sure I looked a most pitiful sight. "You'd best step inside," he said kindly. "We'll see what can be done."

I pressed through the open door without a backward look, and he led me into a small office just inside, and pointed me to a chair.

"Now," he said. "Tell me all about it. What's your name and who's your dad?"

I told him everything. I poured out my story, confident that if only he knew all, he could not refuse me. He was a patient man. He listened right through to the end without interrupting once. "And I know he's a bad man," I finished with a gulp, "or he wouldn't be here at all. But after all, he is my father... and I... I... well, we haven't seen each other for years and years and he wants me... he said so."

The warden rose and sat down at the desk. He pulled out an enormous ledger.

"John Martin," he murmured, turning the pages. Then he sat for a time gazing thoughtfully down at the book, as though uncertain as to what to say next.

"Your dad wasn't a bad man," he said at last. "We were all very fond of your dad... reg'lar nice chap, he was. But the trouble is... he's not here. He behaved so well, he got let out early... left here beginning of April!"

For a moment I sat rigid with shock, as the real meaning of this dawned on me. All the needless deception and fear, all the wasted money and all the dilemma of what to do next meant nothing to me. Only one thing mattered. My father had been out of prison for around two months, and he'd never been near me or asked for me. It was all a terrible mistake. He didn't want me at all. I had no father. I crumpled up in the armchair, and cried as though my heart would break.

The kind warden was quite upset, but had no idea what to do. He lumbered off, scratching his head. He returned with some tea and cake and told me to cheer up as he was fetching a lady who'd put things right in no time. I tried to sip the tea, but my tears still flowed freely, and I cried till I could cry no more. When a lady in a blue uniform arrived (I discovered later that she was a social worker and her name was Miss Dixon), I was lying back perfectly quiet and half asleep. I'd given up on what was to happen next.

The lady seemed more sure of herself than the warden, and acted as though dealing with broken-hearted children was all part of her day's work. She asked me a few questions. Then she remarked that what I needed was a meal and a good sleep, and she was going to take me to her home for the night. Her cheerful common sense reassured me and I pulled myself together and followed her out to the car. In any case, it was a relief to be taken somewhere, as I'd vaguely pictured myself pacing the streets until morning, or perhaps sleeping in the waiting room at the station.

"I'm going to phone your grandparents, Lucy," she said as we drove through the streets. "I'm sure they'd like to come and fetch you tomorrow morning."

But I worked myself into quite a state when she said that. I told her that we were not on the phone and that I had my return ticket and could easily get home alone. For the appearance of an angry Granny in Greening, all mixed up with Miss Dixon and the warden, seemed too complicated to even be considered. Miss Dixon seemed to accept this, and we soon arrived at her flat.

I know it was cheerful and comfortable, and I'm sure Miss Dixon gave me a good meal, but I was too tired and confused and unhappy to register much. I know that by the end of supper I could hardly keep my eyes open, and I believe she found my pyjamas in my rucksack and helped me into bed. Just as I was dropping off to sleep, she put her hand on my shoulder and said,

"Lucy, it won't be at all hard to find your father. There are records kept of all prisoners and we should be able to trace him at once. But you must tell me your address, so he'll know where to find you."

I fell into the trap at once. "Pheasant Cottage, Eastwood Estate, Eastbury," I murmured drowsily, and I remember thinking that there was no point in tracing my father. If he'd loved me, he'd have come for me. I didn't want to see him any more. I hadn't got a father… I fell asleep.

When I woke late next morning I could not imagine where I was. Instead of birdsong and the rustling of summer trees, I could hear buses and cars. A young woman stood at the bottom of my bed. I never remembered seeing her before. She wore a summer dress and her hair fell loose over her shoulders. It was only when I was halfway through my breakfast that I realised she was the same person as Miss Dixon in uniform the night before. She told me she had looked up the Sunday trains, and the next one left at 12. Then she cleared her throat and said carefully:

"Lucy, I felt last night that I needed to have a talk with your grandparents, so I phoned up…"

I stiffened in my seat. "You couldn't!" I protested. "They're not on the phone."

"No, but I sent a police message asking them to phone me," replied Miss Dixon quietly, "and we had a long talk.

They will meet you at the station, but there's nothing to be worried about. They understand now about you wanting to see your father…"

"I don't want to see my father," I muttered, "and I'm not worried." Then because tears were near, I gulped down my tea and went to pack my rucksack and she, sensibly, left me alone. I sat in silence looking at a book until it was time to go to the station. Only when the train came roaring in did I realise how very, very kind Miss Dixon had been. I tried to stammer out my thanks, and tell her I was sorry. But she smiled and seemed to understand that I had not been quite myself. So I waved to her out of the window and then settled down in my corner for the journey.

But the green Cotswold countryside and the crimson flashes of rambling roses against old grey stone gave me no pleasure. My brave expedition had failed utterly and I was just a sly, weary child going home to hear what Granny thought of me. I sat staring dully out of the window until the train stopped at Eastbury. There were Granny and Grandpa hurrying forward to meet me. I noticed how white and old they looked, and the dark circles under Granny's eyes.

I braced myself for the storm, but there was nothing to be afraid of. Miss Dixon's talk had had an odd effect on them, for they seemed to be treating me like a visitor, making conversation about small matters that had nothing to do with the past 24 hours. Grandpa looked acutely miserable, and kept blowing his nose, but he spoke cheerfully. Granny had made a special cake for tea. It was all most strange and I even found myself longing to be scolded.

Don arrived after tea. He seemed rather shy of meeting Granny, so he rang his bicycle bell at the gate until I saw him and rushed out, with Shadow barking a welcome at my heels. Don's eyes were nearly popping out of his head with excited curiosity.

"Whatever happened?" he began. "Didn't you go? I got the bedding over to the stable right under my mum's nose and she never twigged. I went to the spinney and hooted about a hundred times."

"Yes, I did go," I replied. "Come up the hill and I'll tell you all about it."

He parked the bike inside the gate and we climbed the hillside to a favourite place of mine, an outcrop of rock round which thyme and sorrel and bedstraw grew like a garden. There we settled down and I told him every detail of my great adventure.

"Bet your gran was mad with you!" said Don, thoughtfully chewing a bracken stem.

"No, she wasn't," I replied slowly, stroking Shadow's ears. "She didn't say anything. I think Miss Dixon told her not to. But it was all for nothing, Don. He's been out for two months, and he hasn't come for me. I suppose he just didn't want to be bothered with me, after all."

Don shook his head slowly.

"He'll come," he said. "Perhaps he's ill, or perhaps he wants to earn some money, or find a home first, or something. I think fathers always want their children... which reminds me, Dad's going to help me with my Latin tonight, so I'd better go."

We raced down the hill and he pedalled away, whistling. Happy Don, I thought to myself, speeding towards his beloved dad! I sighed and went into the house, thankful that it was nearly bedtime.

Granny came up as usual, but there was still no mention of her opinions of sly children. She kissed me goodnight and then lingered as though she wanted to say something but could not find the right words. An unusual difficulty for Granny!

"Lucy," she said at last, "I'm sorry you couldn't tell us. But never mind about that now... But I want you to understand that if your father ever turns up we will never try to stop him seeing you. You are free to choose. We shall pray to God that you'll choose rightly."

She turned away and seemed to grope for the door, leaving me speechless and dismayed. What did it all mean? Had I been such a sly child that they did not want me any more? Had I run after a love that never existed, only to forfeit the strong love I already possessed? My safe little world seemed to be crumbling all around me, and I panicked.

"Granny, Granny," I cried. I jumped out of bed and tiptoed downstairs to find them both. I had no idea what to say. I just had to get to them.

But on the bottom step I stopped as though turned to stone at a sound I had never heard before. Granny was crying. Between her sobs, I heard her say in a broken voice, "Oh Herbert, Herbert, whatever should we do without her?"

I turned and crept back upstairs. I had found my answer. I jumped into bed and fell deeply and peacefully asleep.

9

We had a holiday on Whit Monday, and I went to see Mr Smith. I found him, as usual, bent over his manuscript looking tired and worried. But he always seemed glad to see me, and always found time to share some new poem or story that he had enjoyed.

"Well, Lucy," he said, "have you come to tell me about your great secret?" He flung himself back in a comfortable chair. I perched happily on the arm, because I had gradually come to talk to Mr Smith as I talked to no other grown-up, without any reserve at all.

"Well, yes," I replied, "I'll tell you now because it's all over. But I shall have to start right at the beginning and tell you about my father. You see, he did something very bad when I was about 3 and he went to prison."

I glanced at him anxiously to see whether he was very shocked, but he only said, "Go on. Tell me more."

So I told him my story all over again, just as I'd told Don and the warden and, like them, he listened quietly until I had nearly finished – so quietly, with his head so bowed, that I thought perhaps he was asleep and stopped talking.

"Have you gone to sleep?" I asked softly.

He looked up quickly. "No, I'm not asleep," he said. "I'm just listening. But Lucy, tell me this. If he was such a bad man why do you want to see him again? You're happy with your grandparents. Wouldn't it be better to forget all about him?"

My eyes filled with tears. This was what I had sometimes reasoned out myself, but Don, and my own heart, told me that my reason was wrong… and I'd risked so much… and all for nothing. I clenched my fists.

"He's my daddy, isn't he?" I almost shouted. "And even if he has been bad I'm still…" I could get no further, for the tears were streaming down my face. Mr Smith pulled a handkerchief out of his pocket and handed it to me, and after a few moments I was able to go on.

"I didn't forget him… I went… and it was terribly difficult… but he's forgotten me. He's been out two months now and he hasn't come… if he'd wanted me… he'd have come quick, wouldn't he?"

Mr Smith leaned forward. "He'll come, Lucy," he said quietly. "And he'll be a lucky man to find such a brave, faithful, loyal little daughter waiting for him. You see, when people come out of prison they are sometimes ashamed and afraid. After all, from what you say, your grandparents don't seem to think much of him, do they? What would they do, if he came?"

"They… they said I could choose," I sniffed. "But they wouldn't want me to go. And…well… he was a bad man, wasn't he, to have gone to prison? And they want me to grow up good… and I couldn't leave them. I shouldn't know what to do!"

Tears were still close, for the whole problem seemed too great to be solved and I didn't know where to turn. But Mr Smith could not tell me what to do either. He only said, "He was a bad man eight years ago Lucy, but eight years is a long time. People sometimes change, specially when they have little girls waiting for them. Don't worry. I think he will come in his own time. And when he comes, you'll know what to do all right."

When I got home the house was empty because my grandparents had gone to a flower show, to exhibit

Grandpa's prize sweet peas. Shadow came running out wagging his tail, and barking at my bicycle. He hated my bicycle because it meant that he could not come with me. I flung myself down on the daisies and hugged him hard, for although he could not tell me what to do, he was very comforting. Granny had often told me to pray when I was in trouble, but I could never feel there was really anyone there listening. Or if there was, he was so far away that my words could not possibly reach him.

Long ago, when I was a tiny child, I had gone to a house with Granny, and she had phoned Grandpa who was ill in hospital. As soon as she had left the room, I too had lifted the receiver and had begun to chatter excitedly to Grandpa. When Granny had come back she had found me crying because he wouldn't answer. She had lifted me on to her lap and explained about disconnected telephones and sometimes, now when I said my prayers, I thought of that disconnected telephone.

Perhaps he did not listen because I had been so deceitful. With my cheek pressed against Shadow's back, I made up my mind to try to be very good, to say my prayers every night, to listen in church instead of making up stories and to read the Bible even though it did not interest me. I decided to help more in the house and garden instead of always running off to play as soon as I could, and to work hard at subjects which I did not like. I would never again tell a lie, or answer back, or pretend I hadn't finished my homework so as to stay up later. Granny had often told me that if I really wanted to be good, the help I needed would be given me, so I resolved to try out what she said.

I tried hard to keep these good resolutions. The rest of the term passed outwardly peacefully, for my grandparents appreciated my efforts and my maths teacher said she could not imagine what had come over me. But deep down, I knew that nothing had really happened. I tried reading my Bible but it seemed an old dead book. In fact church, the Bible and praying seemed like three roads that led into a thick mist which I could not get through. Whether there was some goal beyond the mist or whether the roads just petered out, I had no way of telling. Granny and Grandpa were devout churchgoers who practised their religion but seldom talked about it, and I knew of no words with which to bring up the subject.

And in the meantime the question persisted like a nagging toothache: "If he suddenly comes, what, oh, what shall I do?"

I did well in my end of term exams, and on the first day of the holidays Mr Smith fulfilled his promise and took me to town in his car to change my book token for a book. Granny had never met Mr Smith – he seemed shy of coming to the cottage – but because Don's father spoke so highly of him she let me visit him when I pleased. She saw me off at the gate after breakfast. I remember turning at the corner of the road and thinking how safe and kind she looked under the arch of crimson ramblers. Neither of us had the slightest idea that this was to be the most eventful day in my whole life, and that nothing would ever be quite the same again.

But the expedition started brightly. It was a perfect morning. I stuck my head out of the window, and sniffed at the warm scents of summer, the new-mown hay and honeysuckle, the good smells of farms and bean fields. Late wild roses danced in the hedges alongside early foxgloves. I sang softly to myself because it was the first day of the holidays, the sun was scattering the heat haze, and I was going to town with Mr Smith.

"Happy, Lucy?" he asked suddenly.

I smiled and nodded. We were reaching the outskirts of the town where the cathedral towered rock-like above the shining river. We parked in its shadows, and spent a long time in Smith's selecting my book – an anthology of poems called *The Dragon Book of Verse*. Then we had ice creams, and visited the cathedral, and Mr Smith told me about Norman and Gothic architecture, and pointed out wonders in stone that I would never have noticed by myself. We visited King John's tomb and discussed the Magna Carta and, when we finally came out blinking into the sunshine, it was past dinnertime. So we went to the market and had ham sandwiches, custard tarts and lemonade.

But in spite of all these delights, and in spite of his real love of the cathedral, I could not help noticing how ill Mr Smith looked. He left his sandwich almost untasted and kept coughing in a nervous, worried way. By the time we reached the car he seemed to be breathing faster than normal and, as we left the town, I thought we were also driving faster than usual.

"We're going home a different way," I observed. "Is it quicker?"

He did not answer. He merely drove faster and, after a time, I noticed to my great surprise that our hills, which rose like a barrier across the plain, were getting smaller and further away. Instead of driving towards them we were driving away from them.

"Mr Smith," I said, puzzled but still not scared, "where are we going? This isn't the way home. The hills are behind us."

But again he did not answer. I think it was at this point that a cold trickle of fear crept into my mind, and I became very uneasy. Why didn't he answer? Why were we driving so fast? And why did he look so white and strange? Was I being kidnapped? Suddenly the fear broke loose and I seized his arm.

"Mr Smith," I shouted. "Where are we going? I want to go home and you're going the wrong way."

He slowed up at once and drew the car onto the grass at the side of the road. For a moment we sat in tense silence. Then he turned to me with that gentle smile I had come to know and trust. I knew that I was perfectly safe with him and wondered how I could ever have been afraid.

"Lucy," he said very quietly, "do you ever still think about that bad father of yours?"

I nodded, staring. Perhaps at that moment I began to understand.

"Lucy, what would you do if he ever turned up?"

I just went on staring. Light was dawning... old memories were stirring... not a white weary face but a tanned, laughing face looking back over his shoulder... I was riding a horse... and the skies were very blue... the faces were coming into focus and he was speaking again.

"Lucy, I'm your father. I wanted us to get to know each other before I told you. I've written to your grandparents. Don's father took the letter up at dinnertime. I've asked them if they'll spare you for a few weeks. I want you to come away with me, if you will."

I could not speak, because the thing for which I'd been waiting, half hoping, half dreading, had happened, and it wasn't the least bit like what I'd expected. Only one thing was really clear to me: my father had come after all. He hadn't forsaken me. He'd been there all the time. I realised that I'd loved and trusted this man from the moment I'd set eyes on him, and now I understood why. For a moment, my gladness seemed to be lifting me up high into the sparkling air. Then I came down to earth with a bump, for my father was speaking.

"Lucy," he said, "will you come with me?"

"Yes. If Granny will let me."

"But I don't think Granny will let you, or at least she'd persuade you not to come. I want you to come now. I've told your grandparents in the letter to be at the Roman Camp Hotel at half past three, and I will phone them and talk it over. After all, I'm your father. I have the right... if you'll come."

"But I can't. I must go home first. I haven't got my pyjamas and toothbrush."

"We'll buy all you need. Will you come?"

"But I can't. I haven't said goodbye to Granny and Grandpa."

"But if we go back you won't come at all. You could say goodbye on the phone. Tell them you want to come just for a few weeks. I've promised faithfully to bring you back before school."

"But I can't. They'd be so sad, and Granny would be so cross."

"I'm not sure that they'll be either now that they've read my letter. They knew it was coming, and I think they may be very relieved that I want you to stay with them during term-time. They've done very well by you and that's a good school you go to – you must finish there. I only want you for a holiday at present, and I might have asked for you altogether. But of course it is really up to you. We can say goodbye on the phone and go straight on or, if you decide against it, we'll turn back. I can drop you near the gate and go on. My luggage is in the boot, and I'm leaving today."

"But why won't you come in and talk?"

"Because your granny said long ago, when I took you to them, that she never wanted to see me again. And if we talk you'll give in and stay. You couldn't stand up to them… they've brought you up too well. So it's now or never. Will you come?"

I was silent, and I knew he was watching me as though his life depended on it. This was the moment I'd dreaded, and I felt torn in half. Pictures seemed to flash on the screen of my mind as though it were a cinema gone crazy; little forgotten scenes, all crystal clear: Granny waiting at the bus stop as I came out of primary school, Grandpa leaning over the gate peering into the dusk for my homecoming; Shadow prancing down the path… many more, like strong tendrils drawing me back to the old, secure, obedient life. I looked up imploringly and shook my head.

And then a last scene, clearer than all the others. Don, standing among the daffodils with the burgeoning wood behind him, green and gold, his head thrown back, his hazel eyes very bright. Clear as a bugle blast, his voice challenged me, "I should find him somehow, somewhere, and I should say to him, 'I don't care what you've done, Dad. I'm still your boy!'"

I drew a deep breath and nodded.

"I'll come," I whispered, "when I've phoned Granny and Grandpa."

His tired face relaxed. "Thank you, Lucy," he said. "There's a hotel in the next town. We'll phone from there."

We drove on in silence and I leaned my spinning head against the window, and tried to take in that this was my father. We stopped at an inn called the Cat and Compasses and he ordered tea for me while he went to phone. He was away a long time but when he came back he looked brighter.

"Come quick," he said. "I've left the receiver off for you."

I was not very used to talking on phones and I hardly knew what to say.

"Granny, Grandpa," I cried. "Do you mind? Please say I can go! You see, he was my father all the time… Granny, Grandpa it's only for a few weeks. I'm coming back for sure, and I'll write to you every day."

"Lucy, Lucy!" It was Granny's voice, urgent and pleading. "Do you really want to go? He won't take you against your wishes. Just tell him."

"But Granny, I must go. You see, he's my father, and he's not a bad man. It was all a mistake and he's a good man now. Granny, Grandpa, I'm sorry, but we must give him a chance, mustn't we? Grandpa…"

"God keep you, our darling child!" it was Grandpa's voice, distressed but firm. "Don't be troubled about us, Lucy. It had to come. Only write often and come back. Now goodbye!"

"Goodbye, Granny. Goodbye, Grandpa. Kiss Shadow, and tell Don." I was frantically kissing the receiver, but my father, who was standing behind me, took it gently from me and laid it down.

"I think that's enough," he said. "They understand, and they are glad that it's only for a holiday. Now we must be on our way."

I jumped into the car and we were off, and my heart was in a turmoil of sorrow, relief, regret, excitement, and a wild sense of freedom. The hills and all they stood for were far behind us now, and there was no turning back. What lay ahead I had not yet thought to ask.

In front of us, the road rose to a bright horizon, and beyond that...? I suddenly began to wonder and turned towards him.

"Mr Smith... I mean, Daddy where are we going?"

"To London tonight," he replied. "And tomorrow we must take your photograph, and finish off your passport. We are flying to the south of Spain. I've got your ticket in my pocket. You'll be able to swim in the blue Mediterranean, and we'll stay with your old nurse. She's longing to see you."

But once again I was struck speechless, and simply stared. The day after tomorrow I was going to see the sea.

10

Two days later, not long before sunset, I stood completely dazed and bewildered in the hot southern airport, marvelling at the speed and fluency of the Spanish language that was being gabbled all round me. Out of the window of the plane I had watched the vast expanse of the sea. As soon as my father had collected the luggage – he and I had done some very necessary shopping in London the day before – we were to travel in the bus along the coast. I should see the sea again to my heart's content, and tomorrow I should swim in it! This fact alone filled my thoughts to the exclusion of all else, and my father had to tap me on the shoulder to gain my attention.

"Wake up, Lucy," he said. "The bus is nearly full." We jumped into the two last seats, and the bus rattled off towards the town. I sat silent, trying to take in the great hills storming the hot sunset sky, the silhouettes of palm trees black against the rose, the amazing number of people in the streets and gardens… And, above all, the thin silver horizon eastwards, beyond the port, where the sun still touched the sea.

By the time we had transferred our luggage to another bus, and started our journey south, it was almost dark. But the darker it grew, the livelier the streets became. We kept rattling through colourful little coastal towns where lights streamed from every shop window, and people ate and drank and danced and played guitars and sold their wares on the pavements. Then, about an hour later, the bus drew up in a cobbled square, and my father said, "Come on, Lucy. Here we are."

We gathered up our luggage, and pushed our way through the bright jostling streets until we came to a long, low house a little way out of town. It was a sort of bar, or inn, and once again people sat all over the pavement laughing, eating shrimps and olives and drinking wine. We went round to a door at the side, and my father knocked.

The next moments were rather confusing. The door was opened instantly, and I saw, against the orange glow of the kitchen, a sea of eager faces and shining dark eyes. A voice cried, "Lucita, Lucita," followed by a torrent of Spanish. A woman had thrown her arms round me, was holding me close, and kissing me over and over again. Somehow, the clasp of her arms and the sound of her voice were not entirely unfamiliar... long, long ago... under some very blue skies... We had somehow all got into the kitchen, and she was holding me at arm's length, half laughing, half crying. A pretty, dark-haired girl in a pinafore was stroking my hair, and smiling shyly. Three more shiny-eyed little children were pressing into the circle. My father laughed.

"Don't look so surprised, Lucy," he said. "This is your old nurse, Lola, and this is Rosita who was born the same month as you. You shared her cot! And this is Pepito, who was a fat baby when I last saw him... The others I don't know yet, but you'll soon learn to understand them."

"Pedro, Conchita," said Lola proudly, thrusting them forward, "and Francisco," she added, pulling a sleepy, blinking baby out of a crib in the next room and holding him up. Then she dumped him in Rosita's arms and turned to my father, jabbering, laughing and gesticulating with her hands. To my great surprise, my father appeared to understand, and jabbered back.

So we were somehow escorted by the whole family to two whitewashed rooms at the back of the house opening onto a courtyard roofed by a great vine (I discovered later that it was called a patio). I saw a low table in the middle of it set for supper. Supper also was brought in by the whole family: potato omelettes, bottles of wine, yellow, rather greasy rice with shrimps and other strange morsels in it, and great red slices of watermelon. But the heat and the smell of oil were making me feel rather giddy and, before my father had finished eating, Lola was helping me to bed. But before I lay down, I opened the window that looked out onto the beach, and heard the sound of small waves breaking and drawing back over pebbles. Tomorrow… Tomorrow…

The sun streaming into the room and the cries of the fishermen woke me early next morning, and I rushed to the window. I could not stick my head out because there was an iron grill. But I breathed in the salt, fishy air, and leaned my arms on the sill to watch the pulling in of the nets and the excited sorting of the catch. To me, it was as fascinating as a play. I think I would have knelt there for hours watching the sparkling sea and the busy beach if Rosita had not put her head round the door and pointed severely to my clothes.

"*Venga!*" she said, and signed to me to come.

I lost no time in getting ready. My father, in the room on the other side of the patio, was still asleep. It was quite early, and the bar was being cleaned by a girl, who was singing. I was quite dazzled by the morning light in the streets and the colours of the little town: blue tiled benches in the square, rows of orange trees, scarlet geraniums in the windows, purple and crimson bougainvillea on white walls. Rosita and I linked arms and went to the baker's where we bought enormous loaves. Then we went on to a stall on the pavement where a man was frying batter, squeezing ribbons of paste round and round in the hot fat till it was nearly the size of a cartwheel. Rosita bought the family breakfast. And wherever we went she introduced me proudly with a little bow and flourish as "*Lucita – amiga.*"

It was the first of many happy mornings, for life in Spain followed a happy pattern. Early each morning I shopped with Rosita, and then had breakfast with my father. After breakfast we sat at the table under the vine and read poetry or history or other literature, and sometimes he gave me an essay to write. Then I left him to his own writing and went over to the inn to help Rosita with her many household chores, or took Francisco for a walk, or played with Conchita on the beach. I'd never met such a busy child as Rosita. Lola, who looked after the family and mostly ran the inn, was glad of my help. When I asked Rosita by signs and a few words I'd learned, why her father could not run the inn, she tipped an imaginary bottle to her lips and indicated that he was usually in no condition to do anything at all.

I had dinner with my father. He often looked weary and ill after a morning's writing and seemed out of breath, but he was always gentle and glad of my company. Over our meal, and after dinner when it was too hot to go out, we held long conversations on many different subjects. Only one subject we had never touched on, and I used to think it lay between us. Then one afternoon, when I was lying on a mattress in the shade of the vine, and he was leaning back smoking, we suddenly found ourselves talking about it.

"Daddy," I said, "did Mummy know Lola and Rosita?"

He nodded.

"Lola and your mother were great friends. They were both expecting their first babies at the same time. I was brought up in Spain. My father was in the consulate, and I thought there was nowhere like it. I wanted your mother to love it too, and we kept a most successful little guest house just across the way. When you were born, and she died, Lola fed you and brought you up with Rosita. I gave up the business, came here to this room as a paying guest, and tried to get on with my writing. But I think I'd ceased to care about anything except you, and I didn't write much."

"But why didn't you go to Granny and Grandpa?"

"Your grandparents are excellent people, Lucy, but they had no use for me. They wanted a good man with a steady job for their daughter, and when she married me secretly, against their wishes, they more or less cut me off. I'm not so sure about the old man, but your gran wears the trousers, doesn't she? Alice planned to take you home on a visit. She was sure it would all blow over then – she could never stand being on bad terms with anybody – and sure enough, when she died they tried hard to get in touch. But at that point, I suppose, you might say I cut *them* off. I only knew one thing clearly then, and that was that I wanted to keep you by me. You're very like your mother, Lucy."

"And then?"

"How much have your grandparents told you?"

"Only what I told *you*. I asked Grandpa but he didn't know much – just something about drugs... and that you went to prison."

"Right! I'll tell you everything. I met the agent by chance in a café, although I think now that he'd been shadowing me for a long time. I was just the man he wanted. I'd lived in Spain for years, knew the language, needed money badly, and was half crazy with grief. At first it all seemed quite small, and by the time I realised what a big affair it was, it was too late to pull out. They have their own ways of dealing with defectors. Besides, in a way, I was quite enjoying it!"

"But why did you enjoy it when it was so bad?"

"I didn't think about the badness then. I was so desperate without your mother I just wanted something to make me forget. I didn't care very much what. Smuggling was dangerous and exciting, and I didn't stop to think about *what* I was handling. It brought me lots of money too. I bought a car for myself, and carrycots and teddy bears for you and Rosita." He laughed, and lit another cigarette.

"And then?"

"Well, it all got bigger and bigger till I realised I was involved in a huge international heroin ring. And by then, as I said, it was too late to get out. I did it for three years taking bigger and bigger risks. My big mistake was going to England to meet an agent. The police were after me. They caught me just after I'd taken you to your grandparents. I'm glad I wasn't taken in Spain, or I might never have been allowed back."

"And then you went to prison?"

"Yes, I was sent to prison for ten years, but they cut it down to eight."

"Well," I said thoughtfully, "I don't think it was all that bad. I mean, it's not as bad as stealing or killing people, is it?"

My father became serious.

"Lucy," he said, "to start someone on drugs is far, far worse than killing him outright. I soon realised that when I got to prison and had time to think. Never, never have anything to do with it."

"Then were you very sorry in prison? Wasn't it horrible?"

"Well, I don't know. I spent a lot of time in the infirmary where I was very well treated. But the evenings were pretty bad, locked in those cells, with nothing to do but think. Fortunately I had my writing. I had plenty to write about by that time and that kind of adventure story sells well. What really made me sorry was missing you growing up, and all through my own stupid fault."

"But weren't you ever sorry because… well, sort of… because of God?"

"God? Believe in God if you like, Lucy, but he's never done anything for me except take my wife! No, I was sorry about the lives I'd helped to ruin, and I wanted to be different because of you. You're all I've got now. Old friends kind of disappear when you come out of prison. There's only you."

"But why didn't anyone tell me? Then I could have come and seen you."

"I agreed with your grandparents that it was far better for you not to know while you were little. It's no fun having a father in prison whom you're ashamed of. Children ask questions. You'd never have felt safe."

"But why didn't you tell us it was you when you came out?"

"Because I wanted to introduce myself and get to know you in my own way. If your grandparents had known they'd have turned you right against me, wouldn't they? You know they would."

His voice was hard and bitter, and I was vaguely uneasy because Granny would have considered this shocking talk. But somehow, talking to Daddy was quite different from talking to Granny, or even Grandpa. Granny knew all the answers, and always told me what I ought to think about everything. If I happened to think differently, then I was wrong, and it had always seemed very peaceful and safe.

But this man with his bitter voice and his sad, questioning eyes and wounded past did not know all the answers. He wanted me to think and find out for myself. That remark about God, for instance. I felt all the old foundations of my life trembling. I knew I must think and find out for sure.

Our talk was interrupted by an excited Pepito, as he burst in on us with a letter.

"Lucita!" he shouted, and thrust it at me. It was my second letter from my grandparents. A rush of homesickness came over me as I took it, as though they were stretching out steadying hands across the miles. I stood up.

"I'm going to the shady place to read my letter," I said, and Daddy smiled and nodded. I left him persuading Pepito that he need not follow me, and that I'd share the news on my return.

I knew where to go. If I turned inland and followed a high white wall, I would come to a narrow copse of eucalyptus trees. Beyond were a few tumbledown little houses on the edge of the vineyards and a dirt track leading to a farm, an old stone cross and a plantation of olive trees. This was the shadiest place I knew. I set off towards it, clutching my precious letter.

People who lived near the inn were beginning to know me, and I had already picked up a few words of Spanish and enjoyed greeting people in the friendly Spanish way. But today the neighbourhood was very quiet for the grape harvest had not yet begun, and the children were working in the fields or playing on the beach. Only one old woman, dressed in black, sat at the door of her house with a tortoiseshell cat beside her. She was cleaning a tray with sand and watching a goat.

I said good afternoon to her and then hesitated. Something about her reminded me of Granny. For the first time since arriving in Spain I was feeling really homesick, and the shadow of the future loomed larger, for soon I should have to take sides. I turned back to the old woman and found her looking at me, her tanned, wrinkled face beaming with love. I was strangely drawn to her, and when she moved up, I sat down on the step beside her and stroked the cat. This pleased her, and she turned and opened the door of the house and pointed to a basket of kittens under the table.

I went in to play with them for a few minutes and, as I did so, I looked round. It was very bare and very clean; just a quilted bed, a rush mat, a table, chair and stool, a box… and on it, a black book that looked like Granny's family Bible. I looked at it more closely. It was a Bible – the words *La Biblia* were engraved in gold on the cover. So this old woman believed in God. I remembered Granny had promised to pray to God that I would choose rightly. So, I thought, God was the only person who could help me. I must keep on thinking and finding out, and perhaps when I knew more Spanish, I could come and talk to this old woman.

So I said goodbye, and she stroked my hair, and made signs to me to come again. I nodded, and trotted off along the dirt track where blue stars of chicory, climbing convolvulus and great purple thistles still bloomed in the scorched grass. The farm was surrounded by high walls and smelt of pigs and goats, wild thyme and peppermint, and a friendly, white pig wandered out and began rooting in the dust. I sat down under an olive tree and began to read.

They had both written. Granny's letter was full of good advice, imploring me to wash my hair regularly, to be careful in the sea, never to go out alone and to come back as soon as possible. "We pray for you daily," it ended, "and commit you to God's care. I don't suppose there'll be an English church, but say your prayers every night and trust in your heavenly Father." Grandpa's letter was full of anxious love, scattered among news about the marrows and Shadow, the cat and the church fete, all the little bits of home chat I wanted to hear. I sat for a long time devouring my letters, chewing over every sentence, and I finally turned back to the end of Granny's: "... say your prayers every night and trust in your heavenly Father." ... "God? Believe in God if you like, Lucy, but he's never done anything for me except take my wife!" Oh, who was right and how could I find out? Would the old dull Bible tell me anything I wanted to know? I decided I would try to read it again. I felt torn in half, and I needed a safe place and a counsellor more than ever before, for the great question was still unsolved: who was I really going to belong to?

Today was Friday. Only two days to Sunday. Then Bible-reading and prayer would come quite naturally, because I thought nearly everyone went to church on Sunday. On Sunday I would try again.

11

We spent most of Saturday on the beach swimming and playing round the boats. In the afternoon my father walked along the coast with us to a lonely bay with white sand where we looked for shells. I found one like a delicate pink butterfly. I lay on the hot rocks and gazed into a pool which was like a miniature garden, with starfish, sea anemones, waving seaweeds and tiny whelks. I thought that the God I'd begun to seek must be a wonderful creator to plan such fragile beauty.

We were having breakfast on the little patio and the bells were pealing out all over the town.

"Daddy," I said firmly, "it's Sunday. Can I go to church like I do at home, and can I have a Bible to read?"

"I'm afraid I haven't got a Bible," he said, "and as the churches in this town are all Spanish you wouldn't understand a word. Besides, they're not the kind of churches you've been used to." He hesitated, as though he had more to say, and I waited quietly, watching the patterns of sunshine through the vine leaves on the white tablecloth.

"Lucy," he said at last, "I want you to tell me this: why do you go to church? Does it mean anything to you at all? Or do you just go because Granny tells you to? And do you read your Bible because it helps you or makes any difference to you? Or is it because you've been taught that it's the right thing to do? Think it out and give me an answer. I really want to know. I dislike pious hypocrites, and I don't want you to be one."

I stared at him. Several answers sprang to my lips, but they were not real, true answers, and they wouldn't satisfy him. He really wanted to know.

Lola and the older children had all gone to Mass in a great finery of Sunday clothes and lace, and the bells had stopped ringing. My father seemed more breathless than usual, and I hadn't the heart to ask him to come to the beach. So I sat beside him and wrote to Granny, then I went down to the beach to look for shells by myself. After this we were invited to dinner in the inn kitchen where we gathered round the table under sides of bacon and bunches of herbs and garlic hanging from the ceiling. We ate fresh fish soused in tomato sauce so hot and spiced that it made my eyes water, which caused great merriment. Several bottles of wine were drunk, although my father would never allow me to have any, and everyone became very lively and talkative. By the time we had finished (Sunday dinner started at 2.30pm), it was late in the afternoon. Sunday was hurrying past, and I had still found no answer to Daddy's question, nor any solution to my problem. For the first time I felt really lonely, and my thoughts flew to the old woman with the tortoiseshell cat. I would go and visit her.

"Daddy," I said, "I'm going to visit an old woman who lives just the other side of those eucalyptus trees. Can I take her one of our peaches?"

"Take her two, Lucy." He picked out the best and put them in a bag. "I'm glad you're making friends round here. You'll be chattering Spanish in no time, and I want you to love Spain. Don't go far, and come back before sunset."

I slipped out quietly in case the other children saw me and wanted to come with me. I liked playing with them, and I loved Rosita my amiga, but now I wanted to be alone. It was still very hot, and I was glad of the shade of the trees. I liked their smell, the rustle of their dry leaves and the hum of the cicadas who made such a noise, but whom I could never see.

I walked slowly, thinking about Daddy's question. What did church really mean to me? I thought of Sunday at home – putting on my best clothes, and the cool smell of ancient stone and furniture polish; watching the sunshine making patterns through the stained glass windows; singing the hymns as loud as I could; making up stories and poems during the sermon and hoping it wouldn't be too long; Grandpa falling asleep and Grandma looking concernedly out of the corner of her eye; the happy prospect of Sunday dinner, my favourite pudding and a free afternoon. Did church mean anything more? I could not honestly say that it did, except very occasionally, like on that Good Friday morning when I sensed some hidden beauty in a hymn and longed for I knew not what.

When I came to the houses at the edge of the vineyards, there was no one to be seen. They were probably still all having a siesta and would come to life at sundown. So I knocked rather timidly at the old woman's door, but it was opened immediately by a little girl. I guessed this was the woman's granddaughter. I peeped in, and there was my friend sitting at the table, spectacles on her nose, reading her Bible.

Why? What did it mean to her? Something, I was sure, for when she looked up at me, her face seemed changed, and her hands seemed to caress the book. If only I could speak to her. But as I couldn't, I did a strange, almost desperate thing. I went straight up to her and put the peaches on the table. Then I pointed to the book and repeated the word that the children at the inn said about a hundred times a day: "*Por que?*"… "Why?"

She did not seem at all surprised. She merely pointed with a finger to a word on the page, and I squatted down beside her to look. "Jesus". It was the same in English as it was in Spanish. She repeated it, and then, pointing upwards, she said very simply, "*Jesus es mi amigo.*"

Amigo – it was the word that Rosita used when we walked down the street arm in arm and she introduced me to all and sundry. *Amiga*, because I was a girl, but the same word. "My Friend… Jesus, my Friend…" not someone in history, but near and alive, walking beside us. I suddenly realised, as I gazed at the page, that praying and churchgoing and Bible-reading were no longer three roads leading into the mist. The mist was clearing, and the roads were leading to a bright centre. They led to Jesus – not a person in a book who died hundreds of years ago, but someone who was alive now. He was the old woman's Friend, and I saw no reason at all why he shouldn't be my Friend too. For I suddenly knew that this was what I had been looking for all the time… not words, or rules, but a living person.

The discovery was so great that I can't quite remember what happened next. I wanted to stay near this radiant old woman whose Friend was Jesus. But we had exhausted our common vocabulary, and there was no more we could say. Somehow I found myself on the dirt track that led to the farm, and there in front of me was the stone cross, which had suddenly become terribly important because it was on a cross that my Friend had "died that *I* might be forgiven".

"Thank you," I said, looking up at it, and at that moment I knew what saying my prayers really meant. It was just talking to my Friend, saying thank you, telling him things and knowing that he was listening. It was too hot to stay long near the cross, but I sat under an olive tree and stared across at it and started to tell Jesus things. I told him I was sorry about things I'd said and done wrong. I asked him never to let me tell lies again. I said thank you again for what he had done for me on the cross, paying the price for all my wrongdoings. I said I really wanted him to be my Friend, just like he was the old woman's Friend. And I asked him to show me how to choose, and to make my grandparents and my father like each other so that we could all be one family.

That special mellow light that bathes the world before sunset already rested on land and sea, and the sun was low above the great hills behind me. The stone cross cast a long shadow along the path, and to my imaginative mind the dirt track, illuminated, seemed like the beginning of a new life. I could set out on this bright road, with all my tangled, troubled little past behind me, and Jesus, my Friend, beside me. I knew that I loved him, and I longed for a Bible, because it no longer seemed a dull old history book, but a book where I could learn about my Friend.

The sun disappeared as I came out through the eucalyptus trees, and the sky was streaked with crimson. Lights were coming on in the shops, and the town was waking up. My father was sitting at a table on the pavement having a drink. I sat down beside him, happy, hot and thirsty, and he ordered me a lemonade.

"Daddy," I said eagerly, "you know what you asked me?"

"When, Lucy?"

"This morning – about church and the Bible."

"Oh yes? Have you thought about it?"

"Yes, and I know the answer. The old woman told me."

"What? In Spanish?"

"Yes, and I understood. I know now!"

"Really? Do tell me!"

"I want to go to church, and I want to read my Bible, because… because Jesus is my Friend."

I expected him to smile that twisty smile of his, but he didn't. He just looked at me, and then replied very gently, "In that case, Lucy, I'll get hold of a Bible for you as soon as I can. And if there's such a thing here, and if you're happy to go on your own, I'll find an English church service for you."

12

Waking up next morning was a wonderful experience. At first all seemed as usual: the patch of sunlight on the wall, the lap of waves on the pebbles, the shouts of the fishermen. But then I remembered that everything was different. I was no longer a troubled child, pulled in two directions, not knowing what to believe or where to turn. I had a living, loving Friend who knew the answers, and who would stay with me. I jumped up and dressed, and then knelt down by my bed, and instead of gabbling off a prayer I poured out my problem and knew that I had been heard.

My father looked drawn and white at breakfast and coughed a good deal. But he seemed in good spirits, and suggested we took a bus down the coast to the southern tip of Spain. There I could see the Rock of Gibraltar and the north coast of Africa. And I could have a swim. I was thrilled for I loved seeing things with my father. He was such good company and knew so much about everything. I seized my swimming costume, and we went to the bus stop and bought a picnic in the market while we waited.

I shall never forget that day, and yet I had no knowledge at the time that it was a very special day, because nothing very special happened. We were just happy together. The bus rolled along the coast road with the sea on one side and the vineyards and olive groves on the other, and sometimes a field of sunflowers all facing east. My father talked about the civil war and the siege of the great castle at Toledo, where the general's son was held as ransom for the surrender of the fort. But the general did his duty. "Commit your soul to God, cry long live Spain, and die like a Patriot, my son," said his father down the phone, and the fort held out until troops marched in to their rescue. No one could tell stories like Daddy, and he held me captive until the rattling bus lurched round a corner and I gave a gasp. For there in front of me lay the Straits, sapphire blue, and the Rock of Gibraltar, like a grand old lion couched in the sea. And across the Straits, misty but visible, the high mountains of the North African coast.

We switched from the civil war to the habits of the rock apes of Gibraltar and the snake charmers of Tangier and, as the road wound down in hairpin bends, Gibraltar seemed to rise higher and higher into the sky. Then the bus rattled into the town and stopped near the port where a steamboat was just arriving.

It was very, very hot down there. We ate ice creams under the red and white striped awning of a little café where about half the customers had a different skin tone and talked Arabic instead of Spanish. Then we looked at the shops – at the guitars and castanets and silk embroidered shawls. I chose presents for my grandparents, which delighted me. I took a long, long time deciding on a tile, portraying the Rock of Gibraltar, for Granny's teapot, and a red and gold leather spectacle case for my grandfather. My father sat on a chair in the shop, smoking and half asleep, and did not hurry me at all.

Then we sauntered along by the water's edge to the beach, a curve of white sand with palm trees shading one end. In a trice, I'd slipped into my costume and was speeding towards the sea, dashing into the small waves, falling headlong, and striking out towards the deep water.

I thought that first cool plunge was the most wonderful feeling on earth.

"Don't go too far," shouted my father. I turned and swam back towards him. I wished he would come in too, but he usually seemed to lack energy. When at last I finished bathing, he had found a shady corner and unpacked the picnic. I flung myself down beside him. Then I laughed aloud for the joy of sunshine, blue sea and a strong body, and that other new joy which I'd almost forgotten because it didn't seem a separate joy any longer – just the source and light and colour of all joy. But I could not have put it into words. It was just a feeling.

"Tell me more about that old woman yesterday," said my father suddenly. "She interests me."

I looked up eagerly.

"She's a nice old woman. She lives in a tiny house on the other side of the eucalyptus trees. She's got a tortoiseshell cat and a goat and a whole basket of kittens and a little granddaughter and a Bible. I've visited her twice."

"But how do you communicate? Surely she doesn't know English?"

"Oh no. But I told you, she's got a Bible and we read it together. She pointed to the word '*Jesus*' and it's the same word in English and Spanish."

"I see! And what happened next?"

"She said Jesus was her *Amigo* and I know that word too. Rosita calls me her *amiga*. It means friend."

"A conversion unparalleled in brevity," murmured my father.

"Sorry, Daddy? What do you mean?"

"Never mind. Go on... tell me more."

I munched my sandwich thoughtfully, half turned away from him, because I suspected he was laughing at me. But when he spoke again his voice was quite serious.

"Please, Lucy. I really want to hear the rest."

"Well," I began rather shyly. "I wanted him to be my Friend too. So I went to the cross…"

"The cross? What do you mean?"

"Along the track by the vineyards. There's a farm with a little white pig loose outside, and some hens, and near the gate there's a stone cross. You know, like in the hymn, "He died that we might be forgiven, he died to make us good." And I sat there until I was too hot, and then I sat under a tree."

"And what did you do under the tree?"

"Well… I said sorry. And then… well, I said thank you. And after that… well, I said I really wanted him to be my Friend too."

"And what happened?"

"Well, I walked home. The cross was behind me, and everything in front was sort of shining from the sunset. And I was happy, because now I've got a Friend and I can tell him all my troubles."

"Your troubles, Lucy? I should like to know your troubles too. What are they?"

I turned and faced him steadily.

"I asked him to make you and Granny and Grandpa like each other, so we can all be one family," I said. "That's my biggest trouble. It's horrible having to choose. Can I have a banana, please?"

He did not ask any more questions. He lay back on the sand and closed his eyes, and I thought he was asleep. Only when I got up to run back to the sea did he speak.

"The time's getting on," he said. "Run and have a last swim and then we must get back to the port."

We boarded the bus in the cobbled square. I sensed that my father was very tired, and we travelled home almost in silence. I leaned my head against his shoulder, and gazed my last on the Rock, the Straits eastward, and the North African ranges southward across the sea, until the bus swung round a corner and they were gone.

My father went straight to bed when we got home. I went into the kitchen, and sat with Rosita under some dried fish hanging from a beam, and ate a tortilla. There was great excitement because Lola's brother had come from Barcelona and brought a little rubber boat that you could blow up and float on the waves. Pepito and Pedro just could not wait for next morning and would gladly have set out in the dark had they been allowed to do so. Their uncle was a large man with shiny black hair who laughed a lot and drank a lot, and we all got very warm and merry. It was quite late when I left them, still celebrating, and slipped into our own apartment. The moon was shining right over the patio. I slipped into my father's room. I could hear his rather fast breathing, so I tried to tiptoe out again without waking him, but he called to me.

I'd kissed him goodnight and was leaving the room when he spoke again.

"Lucy," he said, "if what that old woman told you makes you happy, hang on to it. That sort of thing cheered your mother up when she was expecting you... you may need it, one of these days..."

I asked him to explain, but he said it was time to sleep. I went to my room, climbed into bed and lay awake for a long time watching the moonlight on the white wall and wondering what he meant.

13

Next day Pedro and Pepito, in a great state of excitement, came to say that the stout uncle from Barcelona was taking them down to the sea with the rubber boat, and would I like to come too? They were taking a picnic and walking along the beach to the little lonely bay with the white sand, and they were starting right now. Even Rosita was being given a day off from her many household duties, and Conchita (or Concha, as she was known) would ride on Uncle's back.

I hesitated. I wanted to go, but it would mean hours away from my father. "Couldn't you come too, Daddy?" I said.

"Not now," he replied. "I must do some work this morning. My publishers are after me. But I may stroll along and join you after lunch. There's an offshore wind today and it's not too hot."

So we all set off in our bathing things, dancing along at the margin of the waves, and the offshore wind blew the foam lightly backwards. Uncle from Barcelona was so jolly and kept the children in fits of laughter with his jokes and stories and his imitation of a bullfight he'd attended. But I could not understand much of what was being said, so I walked in front, enjoying the beach and the smells and sounds. I loved the tarry smell of ropes, the fishy smell of nets, the salt smell of seaweed, and the sound of the screaming of gulls. I wandered along, looking for shells, and then darted in and out of the water, wishing this walk could last for ever. But it was not so far, after all. We scrambled over the last barrier of rock, and there we were in our special bay long before dinnertime.

The rubber boat was a great success, and we all had rides in turns. Uncle, who was not very good at swimming, splashed behind like an enormous porpoise. Pedro and Pepito loved it, and climbed in and fell out at least fifty times over. Then, exhausted with swimming, laughing and shouting, we drew the boat ashore and settled down on the sand to eat *bocadillos* – half loaves of bread cut across and crammed high with sardines, olives, gherkins and tomatoes. Then we ate slice after slice of watermelon and Uncle said he felt very thirsty. He gazed thoughtfully shorewards and indicated a bright awning in the far distance behind the sand dunes.

By his gestures I gathered that he was going to have a drink and that he would soon be back, and until he came back no one was to go into the sea or play with the boat. Rosita, Pedro and Pepito nodded vigorously. They were good, obedient children. But Concha was not listening. She sat with her back to us, absorbed in building a sandcastle, singing a happy, tuneless little song, and no one took any notice of her.

Uncle left us, and Rosita and I searched for treasures in the rock pools, while Pedro and Pepito went off to roll down the sand dunes. It was very peaceful in this small bay and, being lunchtime, we were the only people there. The pools were fascinating, and I lost all track of time.

Then suddenly Pedro and Pepito began screaming, loud, raucous screams that shocked the drowsy silence. Rosita and I whirled round to see them running across the sand, pointing and screaming.

Pointing at what? We turned and saw. Some way out to sea the rubber boat bobbed on the sparkling water. In it, tranquil and as yet unalarmed, sat 3-year-old Concha, quite enjoying the ride.

We all ran and we all screamed and we all hurled ourselves into the sea, but Rosita realised at once that we could never reach Concha. The boat, carried by the offshore wind, was moving out to sea much quicker than we could swim, tipping dangerously in the deeper swell. Rosita hauled in her brothers and gave frantic directions. They were to run like the wind to the café and fetch Uncle, and I was to run like the wind in the other direction, to where we had seen the fishermen painting their boats and mending their nets. She would stay and watch in case Concha should feel frightened and fall into the sea.

Never before had I run as I ran that day. It was quite a distance but I should reach the next beach before the boys reached their Uncle, for they had to climb the sand dunes and get to the café. I ran unseeing, blinded with horror, for it was all our fault. We should have been watching out for little Concha! How would I explain in Spanish? And would they still be there, and would the fishermen come? And if they did come? Concha was only a baby. Supposing when we got back there was just an empty boat bobbing on the waves?

"Please, please, God!" I cried, and suddenly remembered he was not far away at all. He was the Friend close beside me. I remembered a story from the Bible – a story I must have heard in church a long time ago. Jesus had once walked on the waves. I knew he could still walk on the waves and reach that bobbing little boat with its precious burden. "Please, oh, please," I whispered as I sped across the sand.

"My dear Lucy, are you practising for the Olympics?"

The relief was so great that for a moment I thought my Friend had spoken out loud. Then I realised I'd bumped into my father, strolling along to join us. I flung my arms round his waist too breathless to speak, looked up at him and pointed backwards.

He saw by the expression of anguish in my face that something was seriously wrong, and shaded his eyes to look in the direction of my finger. Then he gave a violent exclamation.

"Go and fetch those fishermen behind the rock, and a boat," he ordered, pushing me away from him, and he began to run as I'd never dreamed he could run. I, exhausted, was left panting where I stood, with no breath left. Yet somehow I stumbled on and rounded the arm of rock. There were two fishermen stretched out asleep on the sand in the shade of the prow.

I sprung on them and shook them, and they jumped up, swearing fierce, Spanish oaths. But I somehow managed to convey that I was in trouble, and persuaded them to come and see. They followed me at a jogtrot round into the bay, but as soon as we came in sight of the little craft we realised that help was no longer needed. It had already arrived.

For my father had reached the boat and was swimming slowly back, propelling it with his hand, while Concha sat smiling, enjoying her little trip. Uncle and the boys had just arrived with a great many other people, all talking, gesticulating and raising their hands to heaven. Only Rosita stood tense and rigid, her black eyes enormous in her white face. I ran to her and took her hand but she did not seem to notice me.

And now they were in shallow water, and my father gave the boat a little shove. It was carried in on the breaking waves, and Concha, like a dark, curly-haired water-baby, came running in through the spray straight into Rosita's arms. And then several things happened at once.

Firstly, Rosita had hysterics and sank down on the beach laughing and crying and clasping her little sister. Pedro and Pepito broke into bellows of relief and the crowd closed round them, loud in their joy and emotion. Everyone pushed and jostled round the children, and no one, except me, turned to welcome the man walking in from the sea.

How slowly he walked! He seemed to be staring at me without seeing me and his face was a strange, blue-grey colour. I ran into the water and held out my hands, and he reached out blindly towards me and stumbled to the margin of the waves. Then he swayed and fell face downward on the sand, drawing great gasping breaths.

He was instantly surrounded by the noisy, excited crowd. For a time, I could not see what was happening. I think one of the fishermen was trying to do artificial respiration, and Uncle was running up the beach. I heard the words "*policia*" and "*ambulancia*" repeated many times, and more and more people arrived as though they had sprung up through the sand. I tried to push my way through the crowd, but I was held back, for they needed room at the centre. Rosita stood weeping beside me with Concha still clasped in her arms. Then the noise died away, and quietness seemed to gather round the still figure of my father. People began shaking their heads and sighing deeply, and every moment seemed to last for an eternity. At last we heard the siren wail of the ambulance, and some men in uniform came running down the beach, followed by two policemen.

They dispersed the crowd in no time and carried my father away on a stretcher. I struggled loose from the restraining crowd and ran after them, pleading to be allowed to go with him. But they explained in a torrent of Spanish that this could not be. The door was slammed in my face and my father was taken away, I knew not where.

We wandered home in a sorry procession, Uncle muttering and much put out, the boys silent and subdued. Rosita, loving and consoling, walked beside me. She seemed to be trying to make me understand that nothing could possibly go wrong once the *ambulancia* and the *policia* had come in on it. But the *policia* had slammed the door on me, and my father's face in the *ambulancia* had still looked grey. I shook my head and refused to be comforted.

When we reached the inn, the children poured out the story to Lola who wept and scolded Concha and hugged her, and scolded the family and wept more. But when she heard about my father, she dumped Concha on the bed and folded me in her arms. Then she sent her brother, who was getting very tired of running, post-haste to the hospital to ask for news.

He was away a long time, and we sat huddled in the low kitchen. Concha played and sang to her doll, and Rosita could not take her eyes off her. Lola tried to tempt me with prawns and slices of salami, but I could do nothing but wait for news of my father, every nerve in my body tense and on edge. At last we heard fast, heavy footsteps in the street and Uncle came back. They all gathered round him in the middle of the room and started talking and talking. I watched their faces and gathered from their nodding heads and eloquent hands that my father was still alive. Then Lola threw a shawl over her head, held out her hand to me and pointed up the hill, so I supposed we were going to the hospital.

The hospital was right at the top of the town, and we twisted our way up many sloping cobbled streets before we reached its iron gates. When we rang the bell, a face peered through a grating and we were admitted by an old nun. She and Lola talked rapidly in low voices, and I sat down on a bench. The afternoon sun was all shut out and I gazed round the great cool corridor that smelt of disinfectant, and wondered where my father was, and what he looked like now. Opposite me on the wall hung a crucifix – not a stone cross like the one by the farm, but a cross with a figure on it, and I shuddered as I looked. This was what had happened to my Friend.

And then I suddenly remembered that the crucifixion was something that had happened 2,000 years ago. It was all over, and death had not been the end. My Friend had come back and was alive and strong and able to help me. I turned my face away from the figure on the cross and thought of my father; that last desperate swim, and little Concha safe and alive and singing in the kitchen, while Daddy had nearly died instead. He'd got there just in time to save her. Perhaps if I could see him and tell him he'd understand.

The nun came over to where I was sitting. She was a gentle old woman with a smooth face, and mercifully she knew a few words of English.

"The father," she said, "very ill… bad heart… come but no much talk!" She laid her fingers on her lips, and I followed her up a staircase, her dress rustling on the stone. She opened the door into a small private ward and glanced in. Then she took my hand and led me to the bed.

My father sat propped upright with pillows, and he had a rubber tube in his nostril attached to a cylinder. His face was still a strange colour, but the loud breathing had stopped and his eyes were open and fixed on me. I kissed him very gently and sat down as close as possible beside him. The nun waited by the door.

"Lucy, darling," my father spoke in a whisper, and his words came haltingly, "are you all right?"

"Yes, Daddy. Are you? You're better, aren't you?"

"A little. Is Lola here?"

"Yes, she's downstairs. Shall I fetch her?"

"In a minute… stay a little longer… then I want to tell her to send a telegram to your grandfather… He must come at once…"

I could feel my face lighting up. "Daddy, when he comes, will you see him and talk to him?"

"Yes… yes… I want to talk to him. Is Concha all right?"

"Yes, quite all right… she's singing and they're all so glad she's alive." I hesitated, not quite knowing how to say what I wanted to say so much. "Daddy, you nearly died, didn't you, so that Concha would be rescued and not drown? Daddy, I was thinking, it was rather like Jesus on the cross, wasn't it? You know, 'He died that we might be forgiven'. Because if you hadn't swum out and nearly died, she'd have been carried right away or fallen out… You got there just in time, didn't you?"

He closed his eyes, and the nun came forward and laid her hand on my shoulder.

"Little girl, come," she said. "The father very ill so you go now. Tomorrow he better. Tomorrow come."

But she waited while I kissed him and he held my hand in both his own and opened his eyes again.

"Yes, just in time," he whispered. "It had tilted badly, and she was slipping sideways… wasn't it a good thing, Lucy, that I got there just in time?"

14

The next day seemed very long, and I wasn't allowed to see my father till 5pm in the evening. I was not particularly anxious about him because he had come round, and once people started getting better I supposed they usually went on getting better. Also the nun had said, "Tomorrow he better," and she ought to know, if anyone did.

Besides, if it hadn't been for his illness, my prayer would never have been answered. But now all that I longed for was going to happen. Grandpa was coming. I guessed Grandpa would come alone, for one of them would have to stay with the poultry. He and my father would talk and be friends. I was quite sure of that. Everyone liked Grandpa, and Grandpa would see at once that Daddy was a good man now. How could he think otherwise when Daddy had nearly died saving Concha? And then, of course, Daddy would come back to Pheasant Cottage when he was better and we'd all be one happy family at last!

I did not know how to pass the hours as I waited for that reply telegram. Supposing it got lost? Or supposing Grandpa, who'd never been to Spain before and knew no Spanish, got lost? Or supposing he had bronchitis and Granny couldn't leave him? Our own apartment seemed lonely and forlorn without Daddy, and I did not want to be there – I'd slept in Rosita's bedroom the previous night. But the kitchen felt too crowded for my restless mood, and I did not feel like staying there either, so I took Concha and Francisco for a walk along the seafront. But the pushchair was so heavy in the heat, and little Concha walked so slowly! I could understand a good deal of what the children said by now, but I longed for someone to really talk to, and my thoughts flew back to the old woman with the tortoiseshell cat. I'd never been to tell her what had happened, and I knew she'd be interested.

I waited until siesta time when, in summer, all sensible Spaniards went to sleep in preparation for the bright, exciting night ahead. Then I slipped out, and crossed the main road into the shade of the eucalyptus trees.

As usual the rustling fragrance of the trees quietened me, and I walked slowly. If I spun out the time, perhaps on my return the telegram would have come. I had thought the old woman might have been asleep too, but she wasn't. She was over near the olive grove pasturing her goat on the rough grass which, growing in the shade, was still a little green. I trotted along the dirt track and joined her under the trees. Her wrinkled old face lit up when she saw me, as though I was very dear to her. She started talking rapidly and, although I could not understand, I knew that it was loving, endearing talk. I looked up at her.

"*Mi padre,*" I said, "*Esta muy mal.*"

I had heard those words many times, on the beach, at the inn and in the hospital, and now they had a tremendous effect. They produced a torrent of sympathy and offers of *pan y leche* which I knew meant bread and milk. I had felt too restless for my dinner, and it had been too oily for my liking, so now I was hungry. I smiled and nodded. We wandered back to the house, the goat skipping behind and occasionally butting me in the back in quite a friendly way.

The house was bare and clean as before, and there was no sign of the grandchild, for which I was thankful. I wanted to be alone with this old woman who knew my Friend. But I said nothing at first, for she was busy heating goats' milk on a primus and cutting slices from a freshly-baked loaf. I ate and drank with enjoyment, looking round at the quilted bed, the worn rush mat, the milking stool and the few kitchen utensils ranged round the primus. On the upturned box covered with a clean cloth lay the Bible, our one real point of contact. She sat watching me as I ate, beaming at me, and I wondered why she seemed to care about me. I was quite an ordinary-looking child, and Spaniards usually had plenty of children of their own. But whatever the reason, I felt very much at home. As soon as I'd finished eating and drinking, I went over to the Bible and put my hand on it and repeated, slowly and clearly, the words she had said to me: "*Jesus es mi Amigo.*"

She was delighted. She nodded her head many times, and her already smiling face became radiant. Then she pointed upwards, laid her other hand over her heart and said, "*Jesus esta en mi corazón.*"

I stared, for once again I had understood. "Corazón" meant "heart", and I'd heard it at least twenty times in the last hours. Men on the beach had whispered it laying their hands on their chests and shaking their heads, Lola had said it with tears in the bar the night before and the old nun had said it, nodding very fast and looking wise. My father had had a heart attack. I'd heard about them before. I'd once asked him why he swallowed so many pills, and why he walked so slowly, and why he didn't come swimming. He'd told me that he had a weak heart, and had to be careful. But when he'd seen little Concha sailing off towards the ocean he had not been careful... and that was why he was in hospital, and that was why Grandpa was coming... I recalled my straying thoughts and tried to think what the old woman meant.

Jesus esta en mi corazón... Jesus is in my heart! This seemed to describe what I'd been feeling. I suddenly remembered my Bible at home, and the picture in the front of it – Jesus knocking at a door with weeds growing all over it. One day I'd asked Granny what door it was, and who he was trying to visit. She'd told me it was a famous picture of our Lord knocking at the door of the human heart. I hadn't been very interested, but now I suddenly felt that a light had shone on that picture.

"Come in," I whispered. "Oh please, please come in!" Then I realised that he'd been there ever since I'd said I really wanted him to be my Friend. He had been teaching me to care more about other people, giving me this new longing to know more about God, and making me happier. He hadn't waited for me to put it into any kind of fancy words, he'd just come to me as soon as I'd wanted him and cried out to him. Perhaps wanting him was the same as opening the door if you didn't understand much, or know how to say it right. I suddenly felt strong and glad and alive and wanted to run and jump in spite of the hot, drowsy afternoon, but I did not do so. I sat quietly listening while the old woman murmured on in Spanish, and though I couldn't understand a word, it all sounded very peaceful and reassuring. After a while I kissed her and went home, for perhaps the telegram would have arrived, and it would soon be time to visit Daddy.

The telegram *had* arrived. The children were running in all directions looking for me. Pepito spied me first and sped to meet me, black locks blown back from his forehead, black eyes sparkling. He seized my hand and dragged me to the kitchen, where Lola produced the envelope from under her apron bodice. They all stood round while I opened it.

"STARTING IMMEDIATELY STOP ARRIVING MALAGA 10.15 THURSDAY STOP GRANDPA."

I read it over and over. Tomorrow by midday Grandpa would be here. With much talk and waving of hands Lola gave me to understand that she had an *amigo* in Malaga who would meet him and put him on the bus, and we would all go and await his arrival in the market square.

I just could not wait to show my father the telegram. Lola had already been up to the hospital to see how he was, and they had said that he was better. So I set out alone, clutching the precious paper and counting the hours. It was nearly 5pm. Grandpa would be here by dinnertime – about nineteen hours – and I'd be asleep for about nine of them. That left ten waking hours and I wondered how I'd get through them. I climbed the cobbled streets slowly for I knew I was a little early, but the kind old nun sat me in her office and gave me a picture book of Spain. And so the minutes ticked by until she reappeared and said, "You come now. The father, he better."

My father really did look a little better although he still tired quickly if he talked much, so I talked to him instead, and showed him the telegram. I told him how lonely I was without him and how I'd slept in Rosita's room and been to see the old woman and feasted on goats' milk and hot brown bread. He smiled.

"You do know how to look after yourself, don't you, Lucita?" he said. "What did you and the old lady talk about this time?"

I looked down shyly.

"Tell me, Lucy. I like hearing about the old lady."

I looked up at him.

"She said, '*Jesus en mi corazón*'. I knew what that meant, because they all talk about your *corazón*. It means, 'heart', doesn't it?"

"Well, yes. But perhaps not quite the same kind of heart…"

He seemed rather breathless, so I described the opening of the telegram and talked about Grandpa's arrival next day. He seemed really glad at the prospect of seeing him. When the nun came to take me away, I skipped off without a care in the world because everything was going to be all right. I ran on to the beach before going to the inn, and sat on a rock watching the colours on the sea while the sun went down behind the hills. I prayed that my father's heart would get better quickly and that he and my grandfather would become friends so we could all live happily ever after like one family. Then, quite sure that my prayer was heard, I went in to supper, and passed a pleasant evening playing games with Rosita and Pepito, and chewing sunflower seeds.

I slept in Rosita's room again, but was woken in the middle of the night by Concha having a nightmare and rising up, screaming, in the large cot she shared with Francisco. She did not say anything at all, and was probably still asleep. She just screamed. But Lola was there in a moment. She did not speak either. She gathered the trembling little girl into her arms and carried her to the safety of her own big brass bedstead. Concha stopped screaming at once.

Rosita had not woken for she was used to nightmares, but I could not go to sleep again for a time. There was so much to think about: Daddy at the hospital, Grandpa probably already in London and my Friend in my heart. Like Concha, I'd understood so little and knew no words to express what I wanted. It hadn't mattered at all. Jesus had heard my "cry in the dark" and he'd come at once and taken me into the shelter and safety of his love.

15

We all arrived much too early in the square to meet the bus into which it was to be hoped that Lola's *amigo* had shepherded Grandpa. Grandpa had never been out of England before, and I felt that anything might happen to him on his own in Spain. My excitement and anxiety had infected all the rest of the family. We hopped up and down, waved and shouted at the wrong buses coming round the corner, and made quite an exhibition of ourselves. We'd been up since early morning, preparing the apartment for Grandpa's arrival, and buying and cooking a special dinner. Although I wanted us to eat all together in the kitchen, Lola had insisted that Grandpa and I should eat alone on the first day. It was only later that I realised that pork chops, new potatoes and early grapes were far too expensive a meal for the whole family.

And then, at last, the right bus swept round the corner and stopped in front of us. And there was Grandpa in his black Sunday suit and Panama hat, peering short-sightedly into the crowd in every direction except the right one. I just had time to notice how very English and out of place he looked in Spain, and then I was in his arms before he'd even seen me. Lola and the children were pressing in on us, smiling, curtseying and shaking hands. They escorted him down the street that led to the inn, all talking Spanish at the same time, with Grandpa, perspiring, smiling and nodding, not understanding a word!

Only when he was comfortably seated in the patio under the vine did we really greet each other. He had removed his hat and coat and had a wash, and Lola had brought him a mug of chilled beer. He said he was feeling much better and took a good look round.

"It's very warm here, isn't it Lucy?" he remarked. "And I must say you are looking well, though perhaps a little thinner. And how tanned you are, my dear! And how's your poor father?"

I sat down and talked and talked about my father: his kindness, his goodness, his courage and how he had nearly given his life for Concha. Grandpa sat watching me, his blue eyes rather troubled and anxious. But he did not interrupt me until I paused for breath.

"Your granny, Lucy… she's quite well, but she finds it kind of hard to settle when you're not there. She's just counting the days until you come home."

"Well, I won't be long," I replied. "Daddy's getting better, and it's not long now until school. Tell me about home, Grandpa. How's the garden? And how's Shadow?"

He chatted on and I sat on the rug at his feet drinking in every detail. I had not realised how much I'd missed home because there had been so much to think about, but now it was all coming back: Granny hanging up the washing under the apple trees (they'd be almost ripe for picking now); the good smell of English baking without oil; the mountain ash berries beginning to redden; butterflies on the Michaelmas daisies; Shadow rolling on green, green grass; the smell of summer rain on bracken. Spain suddenly seemed very parched and hot. Pepito and Pedro kept peeping through a crack in the door that opened onto the patio. They kept being chased away by Lola and coming back again, but I hardly noticed them. I was back at home, waist-deep in willow herb…

Grandpa noticed them, however. He opened his luggage and presented them with a big bag of mixed sweets from Woolworths. They thanked him joyfully with mouths, eyes and hands, and we could hear them for a long time enjoying themselves in the kitchen. Then Lola appeared with the dinner, and all the children came behind her carrying little dishes and bottles. I showed off my few words of Spanish to the amazement of Grandpa, who responded to all attempts to communicate by smiling and nodding. He pecked rather doubtfully at the highly seasoned, oily food, but I ate an enormous meal and thoroughly enjoyed myself.

After dinner, Grandpa had a long sleep for he said he had not slept a wink in his noisy London hotel, and he was feeling the heat. But at 5pm we set out and walked up to the hospital almost in silence. Grandpa was obviously nervous and kept clearing his throat and mopping his brow. I was quiet because I was approaching the great moment of my life. My conflict was about to be resolved, my prayer was about to be answered. Daddy and Grandpa were going to meet, and this time, they would be friends.

I hoped the old nun wouldn't take us up to the ward for I wanted to stage this myself. To my relief, she wasn't there. The doorkeeper let us in, and nodded to the stairs. Grandpa was walking very slowly now, almost as though he were afraid. I just could not wait. I ran ahead, slipped into the room without knocking and took up my favourite position in the crook of my father's arm.

"He's coming, Daddy," I announced. "Grandpa's coming up the stairs now. Are you ready?"

Grandpa's head came cautiously round the door and I wondered, for an instant, just what sort of a monster he expected to see. But at the sight of my father, so pale and weak, propped against pillows, his expression changed suddenly to one of great concern and compassion. He hurried across the room, both hands outstretched.

"Mr Martin," he cried. "How very, very sorry I am to see you like this, sir… Lucy has been telling me about your… er… great courage in saving that child." He had clasped Daddy's free hand, and Daddy was smiling his gentle, pleased smile, not the twisty one which meant he was making fun of someone. It was all most pleasing, and I somehow felt it was all my doing! I swelled with pride and pleasure.

"Draw up that chair, Mr Ferguson," said my father. "I can't talk too much… get a bit breathless… but it's good to see you. Lucy, wait downstairs. I want to talk to Grandpa. Come and say goodbye later."

I trotted away and wandered round the old walled garden, fenced from the sea winds by tall cypress trees and smelling of thyme and lemon verbena. I was very happy for everything was coming right. Daddy and I would soon go home together, and he would get better at Pheasant Cottage where it was cool and green, and great beeches cast shade. He would sit and write in the garden, and I would take him cups of coffee and post his manuscripts. Next summer we'd come back to Spain, to Lola and Rosita and the children and the sea and the fishing boats and the old woman.…

"Lucy, your father's waiting to say goodbye."

Grandpa was standing on the steps, and I ran to him joyfully.

"Did you like him, Grandpa?" I asked. "I told you he was a good man, didn't I?"

"Yes, yes, Lucy. He's a good, brave man. Go to him now, but don't stay long. He's very tired."

I obeyed, wondering. Why did Grandpa seem so distressed? And why were there tears in his eyes? Perhaps my father would tell me. I slipped into his room and hesitated. He lay so still, and his face was such a strange colour.

"Lucy, darling, come here." He managed to lift his arm and put it round me. "I wish I could explain, but I've been talking too long... I'll just have to tell you. I want you to go home with Grandpa tomorrow. You can't stay here alone... but I shall miss you. Hasn't it been a lovely holiday?"

I felt my face flush crimson, and a storm of protest rose to my lips. Leave him alone? It was impossible! I'd stay with Lola and visit him every day, and pack for him when he was well enough to leave. But he pressed my hand.

"Lucy, darling, I'm too tired to argue," he said. "It's just got to be! Come in the morning and say goodbye. I'll explain then. And Lucy... never, never hate! What a stupid waste of time it all was... What a good old man he is!"

There was nothing more to be said. He kissed me and closed his eyes. I leaned against him for a moment or two, gulping back my tears, and then slipped away. As I came downstairs, I could see Grandpa sitting on the bench in the hall waiting for me. But he did not hear my footsteps for he sat deep in thought, with his head bowed and his hands pressed between his knees. He looked such a sad, old man that all my arguments and protests died on my lips, and I suddenly felt afraid. What had gone wrong? They'd liked each other, and Daddy would get better and come home. I put my hand softly on Grandpa's shoulder, and he jumped.

"Grandpa," I whispered tearfully, "couldn't I wait until he's better? He'll need someone to carry his suitcase when he comes home. He's not allowed to carry anything heavy."

"You must do what he says, Lucy," said Grandpa, and his voice was so sorrowful. "He told me in his telegram to book return seats. It's all for the best, my dear. But he'll find it hard to say goodbye in the morning, so you must help him by being brave and obedient." He rose to his feet, and I slipped my hand through his arm because he looked old and sad and feeble, and once again I wondered what could have gone wrong.

We walked home almost in silence, and I left him resting in extreme lowness of spirits. I went into the kitchen to tell Lola and Rosita that I'd got to go home, for there was an awful finality about booked seats that neither argument nor pleading could alter. But I was quite unprepared for the uproar which followed my announcement. Lola clasped me in her arms and burst into tears, Rosita wrung her hands, and the little boys bellowed in unison. Their father added to the commotion by yelling at them from the bar to stop making such a noise. So we wiped our eyes and fried potatoes and had a party. Uncle played the guitar, Rosita danced, and we all sang. Grandpa was too tired to come so we took his supper on a tray. It was quite late before I got back to the apartment. Grandpa seemed to be reading a book upside down and was in no better spirits.

"Grandpa," I whispered, "what's the matter? Why are you so sad? He'll come soon, won't he? And he can come to the cottage, can't he? You did like him, didn't you, Grandpa?"

"Oh yes, yes. Oh dear, yes," said Grandpa much distressed. "But what a lot of time we waste, Lucy, when we won't forgive! I've been sitting here thinking. I never had much book learning and your Granny could say it a lot better than I could. But it seems to me that every hour when we won't love and forgive is an hour of life wasted. And to think of all the years when we could have done so much for him!"

"But you can do it now, Grandpa," I insisted. "We'll all do lots for him when he comes home. And do you think, Grandpa, that when he comes we could go to the plane and meet him, me and you? Because you know, he oughtn't to carry his suitcase himself."

But Grandpa only said, "Please God, we'll do all we can for him, my dear," and went mournfully to bed. I did the same, but not to sleep. For this was the last night I would watch the moonlight wash my white wall and hear the rhythmic break of small, summer waves on pebbles. It was the last night I would listen to the muffled noises of the street in front of the inn: the blaring of radios, the footsteps and the chattering, the strumming of guitars from the cafés, and the mellow songs of those who had had a drop too much. I had spent my last happy evening with Rosita and her family, and tomorrow I would pay my last visit to the hospital. I buried my face in the pillow and felt miserable, but sleep overtook me almost at once. Then I woke to my last, sun-drenched Spanish morning.

There were several things I had to do before we left in the afternoon. I had to pack and visit my father and say goodbye to the old woman and have a farewell dinner with the family. Mercifully I'd woken early – they were still pulling in the nets – and I could pack my treasures before breakfast. These were the presents for my grandparents, Rosita's photograph, the shells I'd picked up, the blue bobbles from the eucalyptus trees (which I was going to make into necklaces) and the postcards I'd bought of Spain and Gibraltar. I wished I'd had presents for the children, but I had no money, and with my father so ill it had not occurred to me to ask for any. Still, perhaps I could send something from England. Then I went with Rosita to fetch bread for the last time, but we kept wiping our eyes and sniffing, so it wasn't a very cheerful expedition.

My grandfather seemed to understand that I was in a great hurry, and he let me bolt my breakfast. We had special permission from the hospital to visit my father in the morning. I was going to visit first and Grandpa would go later. But, once I was on my way, I did not want to hurry at all. I walked slowly for I dreaded leaving him. Still, I knew it was too late to change anything, and the best way to help my father was to obey as cheerfully as possible.

He had just had his morning wash and shave, and he looked fresher and brighter than in the evening. The room faced east and was full of sunshine, and a pleasant-looking young nun was bringing him a drink. My heart felt a little less heavy as I drew up the chair and leaned against the pillows.

"Daddy," I began, "I do wish I didn't have to leave you. Who'll visit you and look after you after I go?"

"Lola will visit me," he replied, "and I couldn't be better looked after anywhere. These nuns are wonderful, and as for that old one who comes in the afternoon – she's right up your street! She tells me she goes to the chapel and prays for me every day."

I turned to see whether he was laughing, but his expression was quite serious and rather sad.

"That's two of us then, Daddy," I said, "because I do too."

"Then keep right on, Lucita," he said gently, and we were silent for a few moments. He seemed tired with talking, so I talked instead. I told him all my wonderful plans for when he came back to England. I described the summer house where he could sit and write, with the clematis and honeysuckle climbing in at the window, and the robin that flew in and out of the spare bedroom which would be his.

"They are longing for you to come," I finished. "You won't be long, will you?"

"I should love to come," he said, "only I can't be quite sure when. But remember, whatever happens in the future, nothing can ever take away this holiday. It's been the happiest time for me since your mother died. You've been such a perfect little companion, Lucy. It was like having her all over again. You are so alike!"

"It's been a lovely holiday," I whispered, because my lips were trembling. "But... but... it's been rather a sad ending, hasn't it!"

He held me as close as he could.

"Not really," he said, "in fact, I sometimes think it's the happiest ending possible. You see, I've often felt sad about those years when we could have been together... and all my own stupid fault. So I'm glad I could give another little girl back to her parents... I often wake in the night and feel so thankful I got there just in time. And if I hadn't been ill I'd never have known your grandfather. It all came right, Lucy. Such a happy ending!"

He was breathless with too much talking. The young nun, who had been hovering outside, came over and put one hand gently on my shoulder and the other on my father's wrist. I gave him a last kiss, and she led me away, but at the door I turned and smiled through my tears.

"It was a lovely holiday," I said in a voice that only trembled slightly. "Thank you, Daddy. Thank you so much!"

"And thank you too, Lucy. Thank you so, so much!" he whispered, and then the door was closed softly behind me. I had said goodbye. Suddenly, everything I was feeling seemed too big for me. There was a tightness in my throat and chest and behind my eyes, and I did not want to go straight back to the house. Why, oh, why, did I have to leave him, just when he needed me to visit him and to fetch things and to pack his suitcase when he got better? Almost without knowing it, my feet had been carrying me across the marketplace towards the vineyards and the olive trees. Each time I'd gone there I'd found comfort, and now I needed it more than ever before.

The grape harvest had begun, and my old woman was there among the vines working hard, her little granddaughter beside her. There were other people there too, and they stared curiously at me as I slipped towards her through the bushes. When she saw me she threw up her hands in delight, and pressed a grape into my mouth. Then she looked at me more closely and knew that I was in trouble. She squatted on the warm soil by her loaded basket and drew me down beside her. The vines made a private shelter round us, and I tried to tell her my sorrow. My father, I explained, with much waving of hands and pointing, was still in hospital. I, with much pointing skywards, was going to England in an avion, a Spanish word much overworked by Pedro and Pepico. I'd come to say adios. My eyes filled with tears again.

She understood at once, and murmured her sympathy. Out of her many Spanish words, there were some that I understood: "Jesus… with me"… "Jesus… with you"… "Jesus… with your father."

"With me – with you." Concha said that all day long. "Play with me… I want to play with you." I nodded at the old woman. Yes, I understood, and I was comforted. In my sadness I'd forgotten. I wasn't leaving my father alone. I was leaving him with Jesus, my Friend, who loved him very much, and who, so far, had made everything come right and answered my prayers. He'd be there in the quiet ward and even if my father didn't know much about him, he knew all about my father. The old nun was praying for Daddy, and I was too, and my grandfather liked him. All was well.

I picked two vine leaves to press in memory of that moment, kissed the old woman and left her lamenting and calling down heaven's blessings on my head. At least, that was what it sounded and looked like. Then, as I walked back with the load of my sadness partly lightened, I remembered something else, something that made me draw in my breath, clap my hands softly, and dance down the dirt track. I was going home to Granny and Shadow!

When at last the letter came, I think I was almost expecting it. Nobody had told me. We had simply stopped talking about Daddy's coming home.

But before that, several things had happened. As soon as we got home, Grandpa told our vicar about my father, He immediately got in touch with an English chaplain in the south of Spain who held services for visitors all through the summer, and he started to visit my father. Then, one day, after we'd received some news from the chaplain about Daddy's health, Granny dropped her bombshell.

We were sitting at the window table eating our dinner on that ordinary September day, when Granny suddenly put down her knife and fork and said, "It's no use, Herbert. I just can't stand it any longer!"

"Stand what, my dear Elsie?" said Grandpa, rising to his feet in alarm. "Is there something wrong with the steak and kidney?"

"Certainly not," said Granny. "I made it myself. It's just that I can no longer stand the thought of that poor, brave husband of Alice's suffering on his own with no family to comfort him. If we sold the antique cabinet I could go and put things to rights."

"My dear," said Grandpa, very flustered, "if you feel like that you must go. But not the antique cabinet, Elsie. That's been in your family for years. I could sell some of the hens. They are a valuable breed."

"Nonsense, Herbert," replied Granny. "I believe you'd as soon get rid of Lucy as get rid of those hens! The cabinet was to have been left to Lucy, but no doubt she'd rather see her father properly cared for. No, child, it's no use looking at me like that because you are not coming with me! School starts in a week's time and you must help take care of your grandpa. Oh yes, Herbert, I know you're very domesticated and all that, but you'll never remember to take your cough mixture unless someone reminds you. It's not that I want to leave you, but when I think of that poor, dear man all alone, I could almost cry!"

She sniffed and almost did cry. I stared at her in amazement. No one had wanted to cry or called him a "poor, dear man" when he was in prison. But there was no doubt about it, something had happened. In short, we had become a family.

Granny was a woman of action. She visited the vicar that very afternoon. He phoned the English chaplain, who promised to meet her and find suitable lodgings. Four days later Granny set off wearing her smartest clothes, with her best tweed coat over her arm. She said that chaplains' wives abroad were always well dressed, and she would not believe us when we told her how hot Spain was. Grandpa took her to the airport, and I stayed the night with Mary Blossom.

I was very glad to see Grandpa back, and we settled down to look after each other in a peaceful sort of way, although he almost lived from one letter to the next. Granny wrote nearly every day and seemed to be enjoying herself. She was actually staying with the English chaplain, and his wife wasn't particularly well dressed. She mostly wore overalls; her daughter and grandchildren were staying with her, and Granny seemed to have become part-time nurse to the baby. She went to the hospital twice a day where she read aloud to my father and took down messages for me.

"But why can't he read himself, Grandpa?" I asked. "And why can't he write to me himself yet?"

"I don't imagine he's strong enough," said Grandpa, looking distressed. And I think it was after that that we stopped talking about Daddy's coming home.

I missed Granny a lot, but it was very restful living with Grandpa. Although the days were outwardly uneventful, for me they were days of great discovery. On first arriving home, I'd hugged Granny and Shadow and then run upstairs to my room to see if my Bible was where I had left it. It was. I'd been too excited and sleepy that night to open it. The next morning I'd overslept, and there was so much to do and see that first day that I only peeped at it. But on Sunday I'd gone to church with my grandparents. Church seemed different. It was no longer an old building where I had to go on Sunday, but my Friend's house, where I could talk to him, using those great words that others had used for centuries past as steps to God. "I believe in God the Father," I said so loudly and joyfully that one or two people glanced round and smiled. Granny looked rather anxious, because she didn't like me being odd. But I didn't care, for the words seemed to be singing to me: "I believe in the Holy Ghost, the Lord, the Giver of Life."

Life! I'd been so near to death that the very word was precious. Concha, tipping on the slippery rubber dinghy... but she was alive. My father, lying so still and grey-faced on the beach... but he'd lived. And the figure on the crucifix at the hospital... but he rose again. After dinner I went to my favourite seat on the rockery behind a screen of hollyhocks, and let the Bible fall open. It was the Gospel of John: "I am the way, the truth and the life!" I decided to read the whole Gospel, and started at the beginning. I read very slowly on into the third chapter, "God loved the people of this world so much that he gave his only Son, so that everyone who has faith in him will have eternal life and never really die."

I looked round. Everything was dying but it didn't seem important because everywhere there were signs of new life. The petals had fallen, but the rose hips were swelling. The butterflies on the Michaelmas daisies had once been caterpillars, but each one had rolled into a chrysalis. The caterpillar had died but the life had persisted. It had come bursting out of the chrysalis as a bright red admiral or tortoiseshell whose wings bore it sunward. "I am ... the life!" I murmured to myself, and read some more. And as I read, I understood, although at the time I could not possibly have put it into words. My Friend was not only Jesus who had lived on earth, and healed the sick, and been kind to children. He was God. And the everlasting life he had given me was his own life – the Life that had created the world and breathed in the spring and quickened the earth. If I believed, I was part of *him*. Then I thought of Daddy, and wished that he could believe too.

A week after Granny left, I went back to school and enjoyed amazing my friends with my stories of planes and the south of Spain, Gibraltar and the Mediterranean. I even talked a little Spanish to them, and their mouths dropped open. I did not say much about my father, but if anyone had asked me why, I could not have told them.

I was very busy helping Grandpa in the house and doing my homework, and had little time for reading. But I tried to read a little of John's Gospel every day. I had got up to Chapter 11. On that Saturday, a fortnight after the beginning of term, Shadow and I went to the woods to pick blackberries, my Bible in my pocket. It was October 1st, and I was happy for I knew Don would be home for the weekend. He had been away when I returned, and I hadn't seen him since my holiday.

I picked the blackberries I needed and then sat on a fallen tree trunk and read John 11, about Jesus' friend, Lazarus, who had died. Yes, it was all there again, death and life: "I am the one who raises the dead to life! Everyone who has faith in me will live, even if they die. And everyone who lives because of faith in me will never really die." I knew Jesus didn't just mean that Lazarus would come back to life. He was talking about his own eternal life. I put the Bible down and thought about it. The seeds fell, the leaves lay buried, but the spring always came again. Those who believed in Jesus never really died at all. I put my Testament back in my pocket and went home, thinking about the apple and blackberry pie I would make for supper.

"Grandpa," I called at the front door, "where are you? I'll get dinner."

There was no answer. I glanced into the living room. There he was, sitting at the table, his face buried in his hands, an open letter in front of him. I stopped dead.

"Grandpa," I cried, "what's the matter?" Shadow, scenting trouble, trotted forward, and laid his nose on Grandpa's knee.

Grandpa looked up quickly and his eyes were full with tears.

Then I knew, and realised that I'd known deep down ever since Granny had gone away. This was what I'd really been waiting for, and this was why life and death had seemed so important.

"My dear, dear Lucy," said Grandpa, "I don't know how to tell you…"

"It's Daddy, isn't it?" I whispered, for my throat felt rather dry. "He's dead, isn't he?" Then I ran into Grandpa's arms and we cried together and Shadow licked us frantically in turn.

"He passed away on Wednesday," said Grandpa at last, "but Granny didn't telegraph because he wanted you to have this letter as soon as you knew. He knew he couldn't last long. That was why he wanted you to leave – he wanted you safe and settled at home when you got the news. He wrote this letter just a little at a time on the days when he felt better. Would you like to read it here with me, my dear, or would you like to take it away by yourself?"

"I think I'd like to read it alone," I said, drying my eyes on Grandpa's handkerchief. "Do you mind if I go back into the woods for a bit?"

"Not at all, my dear," said Grandpa, so I clutched my letter and went out. Shadow, unsure of whom he was meant to be comforting, rushed after me and rushed back to Grandpa several times before he decided that my need was the greater. He trotted quietly beside me, his nose against my hand.

I could hardly bring myself to open the letter because it seemed so strange to be reading a letter from someone who had died. I went back to my fallen tree trunk and looked round me. Autumn had come early that year and the trees, sun-kissed, were glorious in their dying. The beeches and silver birches were pale gold and the horse chestnut a vivid yellow. Acorns and shining conkers lay among the leaf drifts; seeds of life waiting their resurrection. I drew a deep breath and opened my letter.

It was quite long and written in rather shaky handwriting. He told me how much he loved me, and how sorry he was about the years we'd missed when we might have been together. He spoke of Granny, how good she'd been, how thankful he was that we'd all got to know each other, and how glad he was to leave me in such good care. I read very slowly for the letter was nearly finished now, and he hadn't told me what I so wanted to know.

I drew another deep breath and read the last paragraph. "Don't be sad, Lucita. It's the best, happiest ending. I want to tell you that I know now that we shall see each other again – you, me, your mother. Jesus came just in time. The chaplain was a help, but it was you who first showed me. On the beach that day. It's like you said, the cross is behind and it's all bright in front…"

The writing trailed off as though he had been too tired to finish and there was no signature. He had probably meant to go on, but he had written all I wanted to know. A robin on a mountain ash tree suddenly trilled for joy, and I looked up, through my tears, at the blurred gold and crimson and the prismed sunlight. Daddy was right. It was all bright in front. He had passed through death into some springtime of life beyond and, for me too, nothing would ever be the same again. Daddy had opened up to me a whole new world of poetry and beauty; I'd seen the sea; I'd learnt to love Spain and Lola and Rosita. One day I would go back and visit them. And best of all, I'd found out the real secret of eternal life. In Jesus there was life, now and for ever.

Shadow suddenly barked. I brushed away my tears and looked up again. Don was racing through the wood on his way to the cottage, a living, bounding creature leaping over the crimson brambles. He turned his head and saw me.

"Lucy!" he shouted. "All safe, home at last!" and he came careering towards me across the beech mast.

THE TANGLEWOODS' SECRET

Ruth was only good at getting into trouble. Skipping her housework jobs to play with her brother Philip, planning wild schemes to raise money for the camera they both wanted or just being rude to Aunt Margaret. There seemed to be no end to her mischief until the day she actually did run away.

Price £5.99 / ISBN 978 1 78506 288 9

WHERE THE RIVER BEGINS

For Francis, life is already confusing and unhappy. Then, his family breaks up and his mother is taken into hospital. When he goes to stay with a family who live on a farm by a river, he begins to feel a glimmer of hope at last. One day, he sets out on a journey that will change his life for ever, as he tries to find out where the river begins.

Price £5.99 / ISBN 978 1 78506 289 6